OTHER NOVELS BY ROLAND SMITH

I, Q: Independence Hall

Tentacles

Elephant Run

Peak

Cryptid Hunters

Zach's Lie

Jack's Run

The Captain's Dog: My Journey with the Lewis and Clark Tribe

Sasquatch

Thunder Cave

Jaguar

The Last Lobo

I, Q

(Book Two: The White House)

Roland Smith

Sleeping Bear Press™

www.IQtheSeries.com

This one is for the real Heather Hughes

Copyright © 2010 Roland Smith

Library of Congress Cataloging-in-Publication Data on file.

ISBN 978-1-58536-456-5
3 5 7 9 10 8 6 4 2

ISBN 978-1-58536-478-7 (case)
3 5 7 9 10 8 6 4 2

This book was typeset in Berthold Baskerville and Datum
Cover design by Lone Wolf Black Sheep
Cover illustration by Kaylee Cornfield

Printed in the United States.

Sleeping Bear Press™

315 E. Eisenhower Parkway, Suite 200
Ann Arbor, Michigan 48108

© 2010 Sleeping Bear Press is an imprint of Gale, a part of Cengage Learning.

visit us at www.sleepingbearpress.com

Printed by Bang Printing, Brainerd, MN, 2nd Ptg., 08/2010

Author's Note

This is a work of fiction, and there are slight differences between the White House architecture as I conceived it for the story and the actual presidential residence found at 1600 Pennsylvania Avenue in Washington, D.C.

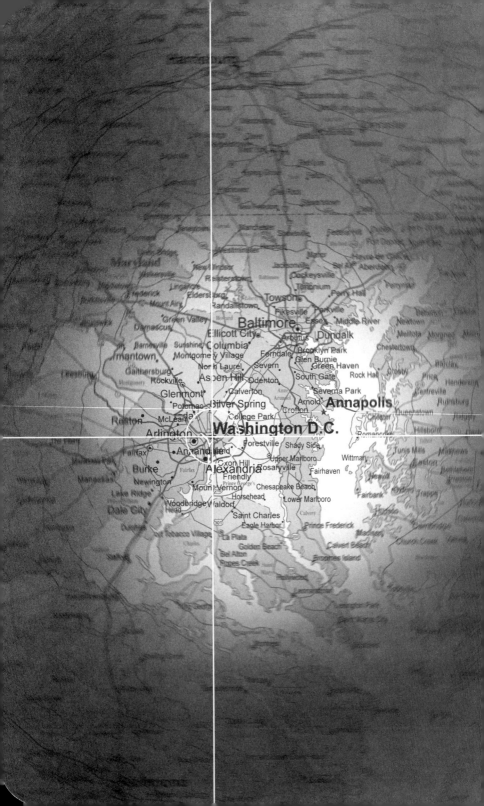

SATURDAY, SEPTEMBER 6 ›

2:00 a.m. to 4:16 a.m.

1600 Pennsylvania Avenue

Boone pulled the motor coach up to one of the security gates of the White House. It was two in the morning. While Mom and Roger, my new stepfather, packed their overnight bags in the master bedroom, Boone gestured me and Angela to the front of the coach.

"Buddy T. and the band are staying at the Willard Hotel two blocks away," he explained quietly. "I'll be at Blair House right across the street from here. The SOS team will be close by. Not that you'll be in any danger inside the White House. It's probably the most secure building in the world."

"Why do you think my moth—" Angela stopped herself. "Malak wanted us to come down here?"

"I'm sure she'll let us know when she's ready," Boone said. "Under no circumstances, and I mean this, are you to disable or turn off your BlackBerrys. We're past all that. You can't ditch us again like you did in Philadelphia. We need to know exactly where you are every second of the day from now on. Is that understood?"

Angela and I nodded.

"I'll be in constant touch with you either by phone, text message, or e-mail. And I expect you to do the same."

Again Angela and I nodded.

Roger and Mom came out of the bedroom with small overnight bags. They were tired after their concert at the Electric Factory in Philadelphia a few hours earlier, but excited.

"Do you have everything?" Mom asked me.

I gave her a smile and showed her my day pack, which was in a lot better shape than the ratty pack on Angela's shoulder.

"Let's go see the president," Roger said.

I doubted President J. R. Culpepper was going to be greeting us at 2:00 a.m. at the security gate. And I was right. We walked up to the gate and were met by a man and a woman dressed in business suits with big smiles on their faces. They looked like public relations people, but the earpieces in their right ears and the microphones clipped to their shirt cuffs gave them away. They were with the Secret Service. I wondered if they had known Angela's mother, and if Roger and Angela were wondering the same thing.

"I'm glad you were able to make it down here on such short notice," the woman said. "You must be exhausted."

"We'll have to run you through a little security check before we let you in," the man said, "but it will only take a couple of minutes."

It took more than a couple of minutes.

Uniformed Secret Service officers checked our identification against the computer they had in the guard station, gave our bags a quick search, then ran the bags through an X-ray machine. We walked through a metal detector. I was the last to go, and this is why it took more than a couple of minutes. I had forgotten to empty my pockets.

A security guy handed me a little tray. "You can empty your pockets into this."

No, I couldn't.

I had six pockets. I always wear cargo pants (cargo shorts in the summer). I pulled out four decks of cards. Three lengths of rope. Silk hankies. Seven magic coins. One BlackBerry. Flashlight. Camera. Sunglasses. Baseball cap. *Goldfinger* by Ian Fleming (paperback). My Leatherman tool (the security guy confiscated it–like I was going to stab or pinch the president of the United States with tweezers–but I guess you can't be too careful). A stack of "special" dollar bills.

"Good grief!" the security guy said.

Four and a half trays later I removed the final item–an origami crane folded from a yellow McDonald's cheeseburger wrapper.

"That's mine!" Angela said. "You made it for me."

"I borrowed it back."

It took me longer to put everything back in than it did to take it out because each item had its special place. The only thing that didn't make it back into a pocket (aside from the Leatherman) was the origami crane. Angela grabbed it from the tray while they were wanding me.

"You're all set to go," the man in the suit said.

"We are very excited to have you here," the woman said. "I simply love your music."

"Thank you," Mom said.

"The president has put you and Roger in the Lincoln Bedroom, on the second floor," the woman told Mom.

"Really," Roger said flatly.

I think it had just dawned on him that he was going to spend the night in a place where his (presumably) dead wife, Malak Tucker, had spent so much time guarding the last president.

"Where are Q and Angela sleeping?" Mom asked enthusiastically, not yet aware of Roger's mood shift.

"They'll be down the hall in the residential quarters," the woman said. "Their bedrooms are not as historically significant, but they are very nice rooms right next door to each other. You can all sleep in tomorrow. The president and his daughter Bethany have a brunch planned for you at eleven, but if you get hungry before then, all you have to do is call the kitchen and they'll bring whatever you want to your rooms. The kitchen is open twenty-four hours a day."

Whatever I want. Twenty-four hours a day.

I was going to order a platter of food with no vegetable matter on it whatsoever.

After a brief tour, Angela and I left Mom and the glum Roger in the Lincoln Bedroom and followed the woman to our bedrooms, which were great. I said good night to Angela, put on my pajamas, and crawled into the biggest and most comfortable bed I had ever slept in. I thought about testing the whatever-whenever-I-want kitchen by ordering a vanilla milkshake and a chili dog before going to sleep, but decided to wait until I woke up.

I closed my eyes, thinking that J. R. Culpepper, the most powerful man in the world, the commander in chief of the United States, aka POTUS, was probably only a few yards away, snoring.

I fell asleep with a smile on my face, but I wasn't asleep long. I woke to a light tapping on my door and Angela slipping into my room before I was able to sit up.

"What's the matter?" I asked groggily.

"I just got a text message from Malak," she said.

I turned on the light and read the short message on Angela's BlackBerry. I was suddenly wide awake and out of bed. "Did you call Boone?"

"I forwarded the text to him," Angela said. "He wrote right back and said that he would be in touch."

"That's all?"

Angela nodded.

"Did you text Malak back?"

"Yes, but I doubt she got it. She probably destroyed her cell phone right after she sent the text."

I wondered how much money cell phone manufacturers made on terrorist cells.

"What should we do?" I asked.

"Wait," Angela said.

Angela sat in one of the chairs. I sat on the edge of the bed.

"Have you been here before?" I asked.

"When I was little," Angela answered. "The former president had a dinner for the families of his Secret Service detail. There was a tour, but I was too young to remember much about it. We weren't allowed up to the living quarters, I know that."

"So, Roger's been here too," I said.

"Yes. I don't think he realized where we were actually staying until we pulled up at the gate. He was still aglow from the concert in Philly."

"Buddy T. warned him about that," I said.

"He warned him about staying at the White House?"

"No. He warned him before they went out on tour about the high he'd be on after a performance."

"I remember," Angela said.

Buddy T. was our parents' pugnacious, irritating, arrogant but usually right manager. Before we left San Francisco, Buddy T. said that if he could find a way to bottle the high Mom and Roger were going to get on tour in front of the fans, he'd be the richest man on earth.

"Even my mom was jacked up," I said. "Can't blame them. They did the *Today* show, *Oprah*, and then performed at the Electric Factory last night. That's a lot of attention in one day—actually, in one life. If that had happened to my real dad he probably wouldn't have remembered he had a son if I were standing right in front of him."

"He'd recognize you," Angela said.

I shook my head. Angela had never met my biological father. His name was Peter "Speed" Paulsen. The nickname came about because he could pick guitar strings faster than any human alive. Speed was also the name of his band, which Mom used to sing with before I came along. Oh, and my dad is crazy, which is one of the reasons Mom left the band and raised me on a sailboat moored in Sausalito, California.

"My point is that Roger and Mom are going to be zoning out on us from time to time, and there's nothing we, or they, can do about it," I said to Angela.

I was kind of jacked up too. I got up and started pacing, expecting Boone to call any moment, but he didn't. Instead there was another knock on my door. I opened it.

Standing in the hallway was a very serious and alert (considering the time of morning) Secret Service agent.

"The president would like to see you both in the Oval Office," he said.

"Now?" I asked. It was 3:00 a.m.

He gave a curt nod.

"Maybe we should change," I said.

"You're fine," the agent said. "He's waiting. Follow me."

I put on my robe and stepped into my tennis shoes.

Angela and I were going to meet the president of the United States in our pj's.

Moles in W.H.

"Moles in W.H." That's how Malak's text message had begun.

I wondered if it had occurred to Angela that the guy we were following down the hall, talking into his sleeve, might be one of the moles.

Mouldwarp.

The Old English word for *mole* popped into my head.

A homework flashback from fourth grade.

We had to give an oral presentation on a mammal of our choice for science class. Most of my classmates chose lions, bears, horses, rhinoceroses–things like that. I asked my science teacher, Mr. Solaris, if I could do my presentation on Harry Houdini, my favorite magician and idol.

Mr. Solaris said no.

I reminded him that he had said "a mammal of your choice," pointing out (very cleverly, I thought) that Harry H. was in the family Hominidae (aka human being) and therefore a mammal.

Mr. Solaris said, "Knock it off, Q. You know what I meant."

So, I chose the mole for my presentation for no other reason than I had stumbled across the word *mouldwarp* and liked it. I had never even seen a mole. I was living on a sailboat.

I realized, of course, that the mole Malak was referring to had nothing to do with nocturnal creatures that lived underground. She meant that there were people working inside the White House who were not who they appeared to be. Spies, spooks, traitors, terrorists...

Angela slowed down. Either that or the Secret Service agent sped up. I couldn't tell which because my mind was mouldwarped, or jacked up, like Roger's and Mom's, but for very different reasons.

"What's the matter with you?" Angela whispered. "You look like a zombie."

"I wonder why," I whispered back. "Maybe it's because I've slept forty-five minutes in the last twenty-four hours. Or maybe it's because last night in Philly a rogue Israeli Mossad agent named Eben Lavi stuck a knife in my neck. Or maybe it's because my body's shutting down from lack of protein, fat, and sugar. Or maybe—"

"I get the point," Angela said. "But you need to pull yourself together. We're on our way to meet the president of the United States."

"That was going to be my fourth maybe, as in, maybe I feel ridiculous dressed in my pajamas, robe, and tennis shoes. And I don't think I've gotten all of the pigeon poop out from under my fingernails."

"Really?"

I'd gotten the poop when we sneaked out of the warehouse in Philadelphia where the motor coach had been parked. Angela's dead mother wanted to meet with her. Turned out she wasn't dead. She was posing as her identical twin sister Anmar, the Leopard–a notorious international terrorist. Anmar had been killed four years earlier at Independence Hall, which was another reason my brain was on override. No one was who they appeared to be except for me...

I am Quest. I, Q...

"Well, I don't think President Culpepper is going to care what you look like," Angela continued. "He has two daughters and a son. One daughter is away at college, and the other–Bethany, I guess–is filling in as First Lady or First Daughter. The president's wife passed away five years ago. President Culpepper's son, Will, is ten years old. Not much younger than you."

"Very funny," I said. "Thirteen is a lot older than ten. And you're only fifteen."

"My point is," Angela said, "President Culpepper is used to having young people around. This is not the first time he's seen kids in pajamas, although the tennis shoes-pj combo may not be something he's seen before."

Secret Service Agent Mouldwarp glanced back at us.

"Brother-sister squabble," I said.

He nodded and continued on, giving us a little more space.

I whispered to Angela, "And this brings me to my fifth maybe, which is, what makes you think Agent Mouldwarp is leading us to POTUS?"

"His name isn't Agent Mouldwarp," Angela said.

"Exactly," I said. "We don't know what his name is because he didn't give us his name."

"He's a Secret Service agent," Angela said. "Seeee-cret... get it? Agents are not in the habit of giving their names out. The man and woman who processed us through the gate didn't give us their names either. He's probably just as confused as we are about why we're being taken to the Oval Office at three in the morning. Secret Service agents are not terrorists."

"No offense," I said, "but your biological mother, Malak 'Angel' Tucker–aka Anmar, aka the Leopard–is a terror–"

"That's not fair, Q!" Angela lowered her voice. "My mother is *posing* as a terrorist. She sacrificed everything to take her identical twin sister's place."

Too far.

"Sorry," I said. "I guess I'm just freaking out a little–post-traumatic stress disorder or something."

"Understandable," Angela said, then grinned.

"What's so funny?"

"We actually *are* squabbling like a real brother and sister."

"Yeah," I said, returning her grin, "even though it's been less than a week since my mom and your dad got married. But most brothers and sisters squabble over who gets to use the bathroom in the morning first, not international terrorism."

Agent Mouldwarp stopped, whispered something into his sleeve, and then turned to us.

"Apparently, the president isn't quite ready for you yet." He opened a door, revealing a beautiful room with antique furniture, old paintings, and fresh flowers in vases. "You'll be comfortable in here. I'll wait outside and get you when he's ready."

Angela was right. The agent did look a little confused, and it's no wonder. If Boone and the president were following Malak's explicit instructions to keep their mouths shut about her, this poor guy had no idea what was going on. He closed the door behind us.

Malak's entire text message had read:

Moles in WH. Terrorist attack imminent. Imperative that you, JRC, Boone, and Q keep this among yourselves for now.

Malak Tucker, former Secret Service agent, mother, wife to Roger Tucker, lay in a comfortable bed on the ground floor of an upscale home in McLean, Virginia, overlooking the Potomac River, across from Washington, D.C.

It was always a ground floor.

If someone were to come through the front door, she could escape through the window or, in this case, the glass patio door.

Outside were thick trees and a trail leading down to the river.

Malak had memorized the map her handler had e-mailed.

The path led to a wooden dock and a kayak.

If she couldn't reach the car in the garage, she could use the kayak.

When she'd arrived at the front door that evening, the family that lived in the home had greeted her like a long-lost sister.

She had never seen the family before.

The family had never seen her.

The husband and wife told their two children (a boy, three, and a girl, seven) that she was a friend of a friend and that she'd be staying for a day or two.

"She's just flown across the ocean," they explained to the kids.

"She's very tired. You will need to be very quiet so she can catch up on her sleep."

Malak had in fact arrived by train from Philadelphia—a two-hour trip. The husband picked her up at Union Station in D.C. He was wearing a business suit and appeared more midwestern than Middle Eastern. He probably was from the Midwest, or at least raised there. He was in his midthirties, fit, well-groomed. Malak guessed he worked on the Hill as a congressional or senatorial aide, or was a lobbyist or a political consultant. But this was not his real job. He was not who he appeared to be. He was a ghost. Planted on U.S. soil years earlier. Waiting to materialize as a terrorist.

The first thing the husband had done that morning, and continued to do throughout the day, was check his junk e-mail. His instructions and assignments were sent to him under subject headings that were certain to land in his junk mail folder. Intelligence agencies totally ignored spam. They didn't even have the resources to monitor the billions of legitimate e-mails for red-flagged words that were sent every day by potential terrorists.

The man had been given combinations of words to look for in the subject headings. When he saw these words he'd open the e-mail and follow the instructions.

Weeks, months, years might go by before he was sent an e-mail from his anonymous handler.

But sometime that afternoon he had gotten an e-mail that read something like:

Pick up woman at Union Station at 8 p.m. Amtrak
from Philadelphia. Red hat. Black leather bag on
left shoulder. Give her a ride home.

The e-mail could just as easily have read:

Return the package to Tysons Corner mall noon this Saturday.

Meaning: place a bomb at the crowded mall on Saturday.

Malak knew all this because this was how she received most of her assignments, but the e-mails were not directed to Malak Tucker. They were sent to Malak's identical twin sister, Anmar ("the Leopard").

Malak had "died" too the day Anmar had died, leaving behind her family, friends, and career. But what she missed most was her daughter.

Seeing Angela in the abandoned apartment the day before in Philadelphia was heartbreaking. Malak had nearly packed it in right there, but she couldn't. It was too late for that now. The only way to protect Angela and Roger and tens of thousands of other innocent people was to rid the world of the ghost cell.

This was the fourth safe house Malak had stayed in on this trip to the States—another address, another piece of the puzzle.

Malak closed her eyes and dozed off. She never really slept anymore.

Sometime after 2:00 a.m. she heard a tapping.

She was up instantly, pistol in hand, safety off, ready to kill...or run. But she didn't have to do either.

Standing outside the patio door was Amun Massri—the biggest piece of the puzzle Malak had. He was young but not as young as he looked.

She invited the ghost into the house.

P.K.

The room Agent Mouldwarp put us in was nice, but it was more a place you perched rather than sat. And it was dark, with only one lamp on.

"John and Abigail Adams were the first couple to occupy the White House," Angela said. "They moved here from Philadelphia in 1800."

"We got here faster from Philly than they did," I said. "You'd think that after bouncing around in a wagon or on horseback they'd want more comfortable furniture to kick back on."

"I'm not saying that this is their furniture," Angela said.

I perched, got out a deck of cards, and started cutting, fanning, and shuffling. I usually told people that I was practicing magic, but messing with cards like this was a little more complicated. The cards were my pacifier. They helped me to calm down and focus my thoughts.

"I guess we should get some photos for our Web page," Angela said.

How she could even think about our homework assignment at a time like this was beyond me, but I pulled my BlackBerry out of my robe and took a couple of snapshots with one hand while I cut the deck with the other.

"Show-off," Angela said. "Why don't you check to see where everyone is?" That was a little more challenging, one-handed. Our BlackBerrys were also tracking devices, compliments of one of Boone's colleagues, X-Ray. We could track Boone's SOS (Some Old Spooks) team, and they could track us. We could also track our parents, which came in pretty handy. And what was even better was that they didn't know we could track them. I scrolled through the list.

"Everyone is somewhere, except for Boone, whose blip doesn't show up on the screen at all."

"Why would he turn his BlackBerry off?" Angela asked. "He had it on when I forwarded him the text message."

I yawned. "Don't know. Is there some kind of protocol when you meet POTUS, like bowing or kissing his ring?"

"He's not a king or the pope," Angela answered. "But I would not address him as POTUS. It's Mr. President."

"I just call him Dad."

Angela jumped.

I nearly fell off my perch.

A kid stepped out of the shadows.

"You're pretty good with those cards."

"You scared us!" I yelled.

"Sorry," he said, but he didn't look sorry.

"You're Willingham Culpepper," Angela said.

"Call me Will or P.K."

"What's P.K. stand for?" I asked.

"President's Kid. The Secret Service has code names for us. Dad's Peregrine. Mom's was Pink. My older sisters are Peach and Polo, but I think their names should have been Prissy and Petty. All *Ps.*"

"How long have you been in here?" Angela asked.

Without answering, he plopped down into an antique chair as if it was an old recliner. No delicate perching for P.K. He had straw-colored hair and alert green eyes. Unlike us, he was fully dressed in black jeans, black T, black tennis shoes. Kind of an elementary school ninja-Goth look. He had an earbud stuck in one ear, which I assumed was attached to an iPod.

"Do you know any card tricks?" he asked.

"Yeah."

"What happened to your neck?"

"Cut it shaving."

"Very funny. Who's Boone?"

Oops. Nothing subtle about P.K. He was direct and to the point. And he'd overheard our conversation.

"You never heard of Daniel Boone?" I asked.

"Of course, but you weren't talking about the famous American folk hero who died on September 26, 1820. He wasn't a blip on anyone's cell phone because they didn't have cell phones or screens back then."

P.K. was also up on his history. I didn't know the exact day Daniel Boone died, and I doubted many other people knew it offhand either.

"I was just kidding," I said. "Boone is a friend of ours. We were checking him on Twitter."

P.K.'s green eyes narrowed like he didn't believe me, which meant he was also perceptive because I was lying through my teeth. I was about to say something else, but Angela jumped in with a perfect diversionary question.

"How did you get in here?"

"Secret passage," P.K. said. "The place is riddled with them."

"Does your dad–" I began.

"Are you kidding?" he said. "He'd kill me if he knew I was wandering around. So would Bethany. They have no idea about the passages, so don't tell them."

"We won't," Angela promised.

P.K. looked relieved, then got down to business.

"I heard you come into the Residence."

"Sorry if we woke you," Angela said.

"I was already awake," P.K. said. "What I want to know is why my dad would ask you to come to the Oval Office at this time of the morning."

Because Angela's dead mother is posing as a notorious terrorist called the Leopard, and she just sent us a text message that said the White House was crawling with moles, and there is going to be an attack in the house.

"I have no idea," I said. "Tell me more about those secret passages."

"Not until you tell me what's going on."

"It's part of our school assignment," Angela said.

Huh? I thought.

"Because of our parents' tour we have to go to school

online," Angela said. "Part of our homework is putting together a Web page. When we heard we were coming to the White House, I called to ask if it would be possible for us to have a short interview with your dad and post it on the page. They said he was too busy." Angela glanced at her watch and gave P.K. a smile. "I guess he found some time."

What a whopper! P.K. didn't buy it either. He rolled his eyes and said, "That is so weak! My dad rarely grants interviews, which is one reason his job approval ratings are in the tank. And if he did do an interview, he wouldn't talk to two kids he doesn't even know in the middle of the night. He does not listen to music—ever. He's never had a concert here at the White House. And he never schedules events on the spur of the moment like he did by inviting Match here. Our jaws nearly hit the table when he told me and Bethany last night at dinner. Bethany was thrilled. She's been playing *Rekindled* almost nonstop since the day the album came out."

"Maybe your dad's more spur-of-the-moment than you think," Angela said. "Maybe he did it to surprise your sister."

P.K. seemed to consider this for a second, then just as quickly rejected the idea. He was beginning to make me feel like a five-year-old.

"Nah," he said. "Not his style. He wouldn't—" P.K. jumped up and put his finger to his earbud. "Darn it. They're ready for you. I gotta go." He hurried into the shadows. "Don't tell Dad I was here. Maybe later you can show me some card tricks."

Obviously P.K. hadn't been listening to music, and what was in his ear was not an earbud but an earpiece like Secret Service people wear. It must have been connected to a Secret

Service radio. Where did he get that? I wondered.

I didn't get a chance to ask him because Agent Mouldwarp opened the door and said, "The president is ready to see you."

As Angela and I walked through the doorway, I stopped and told him I'd forgotten something.

I hurried back inside and walked into the shadows where P.K. had gone. There were two floor-to-ceiling display cases. Between them was a solid mahogany panel.

P.K. wasn't there.

The kid had some pretty good tricks of his own.

The Oval Office

The West Wing was buzzing with activity, but it came to a complete stop when Angela and I walked in. The expensive-looking suits gawked at us like we were extraterrestrials.

I think Agent Mouldwarp realized that he should have let us get dressed because in a voice loud enough for everyone to hear he said, "The West Wing is open 24-7. The world never sleeps. There is always a *lot of work to do here.*"

This got about half the people back to work. The others continued to stare. Some of them didn't look too happy about us being there, especially the group of men and women standing outside the closed door leading to the Oval Office. A man in a pin-striped suit and styled gray hair blocked our way.

"My name is Mr. Todd. I'm the president's chief of staff. Can you shed any light as to why you have been summoned by the president at this time of morning?"

Apparently, Chief of Staff Todd was annoyed about being cut out of the presidential loop. He also didn't look like he'd been awake very long, despite his carefully combed hair.

Before Angela or I could even shrug, Agent Mouldwarp (who I was beginning to think was not a mole) put his face about two inches from Mr. Todd's and said, "I'm sure if the president wanted you to know, he would have informed you himself. Now, please step aside, Mr. Todd."

It was clear that these two guys did not barbecue together on weekends. Mr. Todd gave Agent Mouldwarp a distinctively molelike glower before stepping aside.

Another agent opened the door to the Oval Office, and we walked in. Agent Mouldwarp and the other agent remained outside and closed the door behind us.

Former senator, former vice president, ex-CIA director J. R. Culpepper was sitting behind a large desk. On the desk were two identical red leather boxes. Croc, Boone's ancient blue heeler–border collie, lay at his feet, drooling on the carpet. The dog fixed his weird blue eye on us (his other eye was brown) and gave us a grin–minus a few teeth.

J.R. was fully dressed in a three-piece suit, starched white shirt, and red power tie. He had all of his teeth and flashed them at us.

"Make yourselves comfortable." He waved us onto a sofa next to Boone.

Boone–thin, tanned, and wrinkled–was wearing what he always wore: faded jeans, work shirt, cowboy boots. He had a long gray beard and a long braid halfway down his back.

He looked at us calmly with his pale blue eyes. "Are you two okay?"

We nodded.

He and J.R. didn't seem to notice, or care, about how we

were dressed.

"Ty has been bringing me up to speed about the situation," J.R. said.

Boone's first name was Tyrone, but I'd never heard anyone call him Tyrone or Ty.

J.R. reached down and gave Croc a scratch between the ears. "Did you meet any resistance outside the door?"

"Mr. Todd didn't seem very happy," I said.

J.R. laughed. "Good. I'm not very happy with Mr. Todd either since he's the person who hired ninety-five percent of my staff members, a few of whom, if Malak is correct, are terrorists or working with terrorists."

He looked at Angela. "I knew your mom. I liked her a lot. When I was vice president we used to hang out down in the White House mess and drink coffee. I'm ashamed to say I lost track of her when I was running for my first term. I was briefed about the explosion at Independence Hall and was told that we lost a Secret Service agent, but they didn't say it was Malak. If I'd known..." He let the sentence drop and sighed. "You can imagine my shock when I was contacted by an old Israeli Mossad friend asking me about her death."

J.R. had hired Boone to look into what had happened, and Boone dug up a lot more than anyone had bargained for.

The president opened one of the red boxes on his desk and pulled out a watch. "Do you recognize this?" he asked, holding it out to Angela.

Angela got up and took a closer look. "It's the same kind of watch my mom wore."

J.R. nodded. "It's a Swiss-made Omega Seamaster

Professional GMT, automatic, coaxial escapement watch. Years ago your mother did me a big favor, and I gave her a watch just like this."

"What was the favor?" Angela asked.

"I'm afraid I can't tell you that," J.R. answered. "But I can tell you that I was very grateful."

"She wore that watch all the time," Angela said.

"This is what tipped me off that something wasn't right," J.R. said. "When I read over the classified documents about her so-called death, there was no mention of her wearing a watch. When you saw her yesterday, do you remember if she was wearing it?"

Angela shook her head. "I was too...I was..."

I stood up and looked at the watch. "I can't swear it's the same kind of watch," I said. "But she was wearing a dive watch like this with a blue bezel. It was on a stainless steel bracelet on her left wrist, not on a blue leather strap like this. I noticed that she glanced at the watch several times as if she were late for an appointment."

J.R. smiled. "You're pretty observant."

"So is Angela," I said. "But under the circumstances..."

"Of course," J.R. said.

He handed Angela the watch. "This is for you." He opened the second red box and gave me one just like it. "These watches won't let you down. And I want you to know that I won't let you down either...ever."

I took off the watch I was wearing and buckled on the Seamaster. Angela did the same.

"When you see your mother again," J.R. continued, "show

her the watch. She'll know what it means. Tell her I'm not happy about her modification."

"What do you mean?" Angela asked.

J.R. smiled. "She'll know. When I discovered your mother wasn't wearing the watch at Independence Hall, I called Ty. I didn't think he'd uncover a conspiracy of this magnitude, but I'm delighted that your mother is alive."

"I am too," Angela said. "But she's still in danger."

"Yes, she is," J.R. said. "And it's up to us to keep her safe. The way we do that is to keep this between ourselves, just as she requested. At least for now. This puts you both in an awkward position with your parents, but that can't be helped."

"What about her text message?" I asked.

"It's disturbing, but there's not much I can do about it. If the so-called ghost cell is as deeply entrenched here as Malak believes, I can't be one hundred percent sure about anyone in the White House. I can't tell the Secret Service that I have a credible threat because that might tip off the mole. He or she will tell their handler, and if the information is traced back to Malak, well…"

J.R. looked at Angela. "Did you really kick out some of Eben Lavi's teeth?"

"No," she answered. "I loosened a couple."

Eben Lavi was a rogue Mossad agent who was now working with SOS. We hoped.

J.R. smiled. "Theodore Roosevelt built the West Wing in 1902. If he were sitting where I'm sitting right now, he would say, 'Bully!' "

He looked back at me. "And I understand that you pulled

a fast one on Lavi with a magic trick at the hospital."

"It was no big deal."

"That's not what I hear," J.R. said. "The reason I had you come down is that I wanted to meet you and thank you personally. I might not have time later. Since I can't tell my Secret Service detail about the alleged attack, and I have to assume I'm the target, I'm going to have to change my appointments at the last minute to stay ahead of the ghost cell. It'll be a confusing day for my staff, but it will keep them on their toes. I've done this before, so hopefully it won't look like I've been tipped off." He chuckled. "They'll just think that I've lost my mind...again.

"And I have another favor to ask. When you meet my son, Will, if you haven't already, I'd appreciate it if you spent some time with him. He gets a little stir-crazy and lonesome cooped up in this place. It's hard living inside a glass house. And having me as a dad hasn't been easy for him."

Having a mom like Malak hadn't been easy for Angela either. Will seemed to have adjusted pretty well to becoming the P.K.

J.R. gave Croc a final scratch between the ears and then stood.

That's it? I thought.

He walked over and shook our hands. "I'll go out the main door," he said. "This is your house. I've instructed Agent Norton to give you free rein."

"Who's Agent Norton?" Angela asked.

"The agent who led you down here."

"What if he's one of the moles?" I asked.

"I seriously doubt that, but you don't have to worry about it. He doesn't know what's going on. All he knows is that he's supposed to keep an eye on you."

Aka babysit. I wondered what Agent Mouldwarp Norton thought about that.

"When you see your mother, give her my regards," J.R. said. "Tell her that when this is all over, I want her to visit me. I'll buy her a cup of coffee in the White House mess, for old times' sake."

I didn't think this would ever be over for Malak.

J.R. opened the thick door and walked past Agent Norton into the hive.

Plausible Deniability

"What was that about?" Angela asked.

I looked at the Seamaster. "That was about five minutes."

"You're hilarious, Q."

"Thanks, sis."

"Don't call me sis."

"I think he invited you down here just to meet you," Boone said. "And to rattle his staff. That's why he paraded you into the Oval Office rather than meet with you privately up in the Residence. J.R. has never been known for being subtle. When I worked for him at the CIA, he'd pull this kind of stunt all the time to test his staff's reactions. When I passed on Malak's warning to him he could have just as easily called in the FBI, the Secret Service, the National Security Agency, the Department of Defense, Homeland Security, and the CIA. That's what most presidents would have done. And that would have been a huge blunder. All we have—all he has—is Malak. He's risking his life to protect her cover. Impressive. Do you have your BlackBerrys?"

We pulled them out of our pockets.

Boone reached into his tattered day pack. "Change of equipment." He pulled out two iPhones and chargers. "X-Ray put his special touch on these. They have all the same functions as your BlackBerrys."

"Why the switch?" I asked. We'd had our BlackBerrys less than three days.

"There are some things these do that the BlackBerry doesn't do," Boone answered. "If they work well we might all switch."

The iPhones *were* a lot cooler.

Angela flipped hers over and smiled. "No way to take the battery out," she said.

"Really?" Boone said innocently.

"Like you and X-Ray didn't know that," Angela said.

In Philly she'd ditched Felix, the SOS guy guarding her, and then pulled the BlackBerry battery so the team couldn't find her.

"That's one of the things the iPhone has that the BlackBerry doesn't have," Boone said.

"Speaking of which," Angela said, "Q did a location check on everyone before we came down here, and you didn't show up."

"I pulled the battery," Boone said with a grin. "I didn't want anyone to know I was here. J.R. smuggled me in. Ziv and Dirk hacked into our computer system in Philly. X-Ray thinks it might still be compromised. He's working on the problem, but it's going to take a while for him to fix it. In the meantime we have to be very careful. Politically, J.R. can't afford to be associated with an off-the-books covert operation like this. If it goes sour he needs to have plausible deniability."

"What's that?" I asked.

Of course Angela knew. "It means that there can be no record of Boone or the other members of SOS speaking to the president."

Boone nodded. "When I got your text message I called J.R. from a disposable cell. I tried to talk him out of a face-to-face meeting, but he insisted. Halfway through my briefing he called Agent Norton and asked him to bring you two down here."

"Why?" I asked.

"Like he said, I think he wanted to shake up his staff. Set the stage for his crazy act later today. During the briefing I tried to downplay your antics in Philly, but J.R. read between the lines and insisted you come down." Boone smiled. "But he knew he was going to do it all along. The Omegas were on his desk when I came in."

"What do you want us to do?" Angela asked.

"I would like to have you do absolutely nothing," Boone said, then sighed. "But that's probably too much to hope for, right?"

"Probably," I answered.

"Definitely," Angela said.

"That's what I thought. Since this is your *home* and J.R. is giving you *free* rein, I guess we should put this to some use. I don't want either of you to look for the moles actively, but I want you to keep your eyes open and let us know what's going on inside the house. You're going to be approached by staff asking you why the president invited you down here. One or more of them is likely to be the mole. You need to be friendly and innocent, like kids, which I know is going to be a stretch for both of you. If you meet someone whom you think is acting suspiciously, text the name to X-Ray. He'll run it through our database to see if he gets any bad-guy hits. Before you talk to anybody you need to come up with a plausible story about why J.R. invited you down here in your pajamas."

So, he had noticed the pj's.

Angela gave Boone the same whopper she had given P.K., without mentioning the fact that we had met the President's Kid.

"Perfect!" Boone stood and shouldered his pack. "I have to sneak back out of here, and you two need to get some sleep. Keep those phones charged and with you at all times."

He walked over to a door near J.R.'s desk, opened it, and disappeared with Croc at his boot heels.

"I noticed you didn't tell him about P.K.," I said.

"We told P.K. we wouldn't tell. I didn't think it was important. He's just a kid."

P.K. was not just a kid, but I let it go.

Angela stood and yawned. "I'm exhausted." She started toward the door we'd entered through.

"Wait."

"What?"

"I think Mr. Todd's going to be on the other side of that door, or one of his cronies. They're going to ask us why the president of the United States left two kids in the Oval Office on their own."

"Good point," Angela said. "What are we going to tell them?"

I walked behind J.R.'s desk and sat down in his chair. I'm sure it was my imagination, but as soon as my butt hit that seat I felt a surge of power pulsate into every cell in my body.

"Wow!"

"POTUS," Angela said. "*Pajamas* of the United States. What are we going to tell Mr. Todd?"

"I have given it careful thought," I said, trying to sound presidential. "And I have decided that we will tell the chief of staff that J.R. left us alone for a few minutes so I could play president."

"Works for me," Angela said. "Now let's get some sleep."

Tyrone Boone, former spy, ex-rock band roadie, motor coach chauffeur, de facto leader of SOS, crossed the street from the White House to Lafayette Park. A row of perpetual protesters lined the sidewalk, curled up in blankets and sleeping bags. But not all of them were protesters. Among the bedraggled group were undercover FBI and Secret Service agents posing as disenfranchised citizens. And not all of them were asleep.

"Thirsty?" A man held up a bottle wrapped in a brown paper bag.

"Who'd you tick off?" Boone asked.

"Boone? Tyrone Boone? I can't believe it!"

"Then you must be suffering from short-term memory loss, Pat," Boone said. "About three minutes ago your cohorts across the street told you that I had just walked past the White House and was heading your way. When you saw me approaching you whispered up your sleeve that you had acquired the target."

Pat smiled. "Have a seat."

Boone sat down on a lawn chair, sniffed the open bottle, wrinkled his nose, and handed it back. "So, who did you tick off, Pat?"

Pat sighed. "Everybody."

"Some things never change," Boone said. "How long have you had this duty?"

"Thirteen months, going on eternity. It's not as bad as it looks... or smells. I like a lot of these people. Some of them are pretty bright and have legitimate gripes."

Boone had known Patrick James Callaghan for more than thirty years. Pat was one of a handful of people that knew Boone had been a NOC (nonofficial cover) CIA agent. They'd worked together in Europe and the Middle East. Pat was a good agent but got into trouble—like most good agents do. The CIA gave him the boot, and he joined the Secret Service.

"Sounds like you've been radicalized," Boone said.

Pat laughed. "Not any more than I already was. How's the old man?"

"I wouldn't know," Boone said. "I haven't seen J.R. in years and doubt he'd remember me. I've been out of the trade for over a decade now. I couldn't sleep and went for a late-night walk. Stopped by the gate and asked a Secret Service uniform to make a call to check if the kids I'm watching were tucked in for the night."

"They put you in nice digs," Pat said. "Blair House is for visiting dignitaries and heads of state, not roadies. And I understand the band is at the Willard."

"I'm the driver. And they decided to put me in charge of security. The parents didn't want me or my security crew too far from their kids. The White House nixed our staying in the mansion, but Blair House is pretty darn comfortable."

Pat laughed. "I knew you'd have an answer, Boone. You always do. But what do you think of those two kids getting a private audience with the president of the United States at three o'clock in the morning?"

"They did?" Boone said. "I knew they were trying to get an interview with him for their school assignment. I guess J.R. was awake and decided to give them some time."

Pat pulled out his earpiece from under his long, greasy hair, took his radio from his back pocket, and turned it off. "Okay, I'm off the clock," he said. "What's going on, Boone? What are you doing?"

"You guys are never off the clock," Boone said. "There is nothing going on. And what I do is none of your business, Pat."

"You're right, but I had to ask. Someone said he thought he spotted you coming out of the Executive Building, next door to the White House."

"The mythical presidential tunnel?" Boone said.

"Yeah."

"Well, I've never been in that tunnel, and I didn't come out of that building."

Pat nodded toward the White House. "They're going crazy over there. J.R. is having another one of his meltdowns."

"I don't know anything about that either. You've known him as long as I have. Meltdowns are standard operating procedure for J.R. He's crazy like a fox."

"Did you know that the girl's mother was Malak Tucker?"

Boone nodded.

"Did you ever meet her?"

"Once," Boone answered. "When she was on the protection detail in the White House. I was there for a briefing. She patted me down after I went through the metal detector. Guess she didn't like me."

"If you could just give me a little nugget," Pat said, "I might be able to get off the street and back into the big show."

"If I had a little nugget to give you, Pat, I would. You're a good agent. You don't deserve to be on homeless duty. And I think you could get back into the White House all on your own with a single phone call."

"Probably," Pat admitted. "But I won't make that call. It wouldn't be right."

Boone stood.

"One more thing," Pat said, joining him. "About a year ago I heard this wild rumor."

"Yeah?"

"Someone told me that a group of old ex-spooks had gotten together and were doing off-the-book missions."

"If that's true, then they're crazy. Thirty years was thirty years too long for me. I'm enjoying my retirement. There isn't enough money in the world to bring me out of it."

Pat knelt down and scratched Croc between the ears. "Good grief, your dog looks just like your old dog. How'd you manage that?"

"Same genes," Boone said.

Pat stood back up. "Well, if you ever hear anything about the old spooks, put in a good word for me. I wouldn't mind joining them."

"If they exist, I'd be the last person they'd contact."

Boone walked off into the night past the statue of Andrew Jackson on horseback waving his hat, wondering where Pat had heard the rumor.

SATURDAY, SEPTEMBER 6 >

4:10 a.m. to 8:51 a.m.

Silver Bullet

I didn't think I'd be able to sleep, so when I got back to the room I tried the kitchen's twenty-four-hour-whatever-I-want-sent-to-my-room thing by ordering a vanilla shake and fries.

The guy on the other end of the line—the graveyard chef, I guess—said, "Good morning, Mr. Tucker. How may I help you?"

"I'd like a vanilla shake and some fries."

"Perfection! But I would recommend my deep-fried cheese curds. They are one of my specialties."

"What's a cheese curd?"

"Cheese before it becomes cheese."

"Okay, I'll try them."

"Perfection! You won't be sorry. I'll have that up to your room in about twenty minutes."

I don't know if the curds made it to my room in twenty minutes or not, because I fell asleep about five minutes after I placed the order. When I woke up there was a melted vanilla milkshake and a congealed pile of deep-fried cheese curds on the table.

Sitting next to the midnight snack was P.K.

"Morning," he said.

I sat up. "How'd you get in here?"

"Your door was open."

I remembered. I'd left it open for the fried curds.

P.K. looked at the food. "That stuff will kill you."

I swung my legs out of bed. "What are you, a health nut?"

"Nah, I've had a ton of Chef Cheesy's specialty—at least when Bethany isn't around. She's a food cop."

"I hear you."

Roger was a vegetarian, and Mom was trying to become one, and they were taking me along for the ride. Luckily, Angela was a closet carnivore. The curds weren't meat, but by the looks of them they were fried in animal fat, which was not allowed.

"You call him Chef Cheesy?"

"He calls himself Chef Cheesy," P.K. answered. "His real name's Conrad Fournier. He graduated from the Le Cordon Bleu culinary school in Paris, but he was born and raised in Milwaukee. He's been here about five years. Dad hired him over the objections of just about everyone in the house. Now everybody loves him. Especially the Secret Service because he sneaks them food 24-7. He weighs about a hundred pounds, which is weird considering how much cheese he eats. But his nickname doesn't come from cheese consumption. It comes from his cheesy jokes, not curds. Dad loves cheesy jokes. Bethany calls him Chef Cholesterol. I eat in the kitchen with him all the time. He's probably the best friend I have in the house."

"How many people work in the White House?" I asked.

"My dad says about *half* of them," P.K. answered.

"Funny," I said.

"I don't know exactly how many work here," P.K. said. "Dad has over a hundred and fifty people working for him in the West Wing. Then there are close to a hundred people working in the East Wing on First Lady things with Bethany. Then there's the household staff... There are probably a couple hundred of them. Secret Service, S.S. Uniformed Division, army, navy, marine, air force, Countersniper Support Unit, Emergency Response Team, canine officers... Is this for your school assignment?"

"Yeah," I said.

Actually, I'd asked in order to get some idea of how hard it would be for a mole to infiltrate the White House.

Answer: easy.

"How did the interview go with my dad?"

"It was brief," I said. "But it was nice of him to make time for us."

"Everybody's talking about it."

Which reminded me... I pulled out my iPhone to see if there were any horrible text messages or voice mails. There weren't. Four hours without a major disaster. It might turn out to be a good day.

"Hey!" P.K. said. "I thought you had a BlackBerry last night."

Oops.

"Nope," I lied. "An iPhone. BlackBerrys are very uncool.

I wouldn't disgrace my pocket with one."

P.K. narrowed his green eyes. "I could have sworn–"

"I'm starving," I said. "Where do I get breakfast?"

"You can have it brought to your room, or you can eat in the Residence kitchen or the dining room or up in the Solarium."

"The Solarium?"

"Top floor. Aside from the kitchen it's my favorite place to hang out."

"Then that's where I want to eat," I said.

P.K. smiled.

I hoped he had forgotten about the BlackBerry.

"Let's get back to that BlackBerry."

Guess he hadn't forgotten. Silver bullet time.

"That reminds me," I said. "Where did you get the Secret Service radio?"

P.K.'s eyes went wide. "What are you talking about?"

"And how did you learn about the secret passage?"

"I thought you said you were hungry," P.K. said.

"I am. Why don't you see if Angela's up while I take a shower and get dressed."

P.K. was out of the room like a silver bullet.

Solarium

Solarium was a fancy name for sunroom, but I saw why P.K. liked it up there. It was bright and cheerful.

"President Coolidge's wife called this room her sky parlor," Angela said as she strolled in, looking pretty cheerful despite everything that was going on. She set her pack on the table. "Did you take any photos for the Web page?"

P.K. and I were sitting at a long table, and I was showing him a couple of simple card tricks.

"A few," I said. "And I shot some video too."

"You did not," P.K. said.

I showed him the photos and short video clip on my iPhone. "You weren't paying attention," I said. "Remember what I was telling you about sleight of hand? You thought I was just holding my phone in my hand when we came in here, but what I was really doing was taking photos and video."

And they were pretty good, considering I'd messed around with the new phone for only about twenty minutes. I thought P.K. was going to bring up the BlackBerry question again, but he didn't. I guessed I'd shot that subject down.

P.K. walked over to one of the house phones. "What do you want for breakfast?"

I knew what I wanted, but I didn't know if I could have it. I looked at Angela. "Have you seen Mom or Roger?"

She shook her head. I could just see the reaction on their faces if they strolled into the Solarium and saw the pile of sizzling bacon and sausages on the platter I was going to order.

"Bethany has them in the East Wing," P.K. said. "They're talking about the concert tonight. When they finish in the East Wing there's the brunch, which you definitely don't want to go to."

"Why not?" Angela asked.

"When they hold a brunch for you, you don't get to eat because everyone is talking to you."

"I'd like three eggs over easy, bacon, sausage, burned hash browns, toast, and a big glass of milk."

"Make that two," Angela said.

"Bethany said you were all vegetarians," P.K. said.

"We are," Angela said. "When we're with our parents."

P.K. grinned. "I get it."

He placed the order.

The food arrived within minutes, wheeled in by a server named Maurice wearing a snow-white waistcoat, starched shirt, black pants, black tie, and a big smile. It was obvious that he was very fond of P.K.

"I was told our guests were vegetarians, P.K.," Maurice said as he set down the plates.

"Don't tell anyone," P.K. said.

"Your secret is safe." Maurice looked at Angela and me. "P.K. and I have a sacred pact. I don't say anything to anyone about what he's up to unless I think he's endangering himself. Even then I talk to him about it first. I believe the same should apply to his friends."

"Has he ever endangered himself?" Angela asked.

"That is strictly between me and P.K." Maurice gave us another dazzling smile and wheeled the serving cart out of the room.

The breakfast was perfection, as Chef Cheesy would say.

Just as I forked the last slice of sausage into my mouth, my iPhone rang.

"Hi, Mom."

"What are you doing?"

"We're up in the Solarium with the First Son, eating breakfast."

"What are you having?"

"Fruit, granola, yogurt, cucumber juice…"

"I'll bet," Mom said.

"Here's a tip for you. You'd better get something to eat now because you won't be able to eat at the brunch because you'll be too busy jabbering with fans."

"Roger and I know the routine. We've already eaten. And unlike you, we actually had fruit, granola, and yogurt. You should probably be more sensitive toward Angela. I'm sure she isn't fond of watching you wolf down dead animals."

I looked across the table at Angela. She was dipping her last piece of bacon in the yoke of her last egg.

"You're right," I said. "She's revolted."

"Put her on," Mom said. "Roger would like to talk to her."

I looked at Angela's greasy fingers and decided to put her on speakerphone.

"Hi, Dad," Angela said.

"Hi, honey. How's it going?"

"Great."

"I hear you had a surprise audience with the president early this morning."

No secrets in the White House, I thought.

"We did. It was great and very nice of him to make time for us."

"I didn't know you'd contacted the White House office to ask for an interview."

"I didn't think he'd grant one," Angela said. "Boone made the call for us."

"Good old Boone," Roger said.

He sounded a lot more up than he had the night before.

"Are you coming to the brunch?" he asked.

"We're pretty tired," Angela answered. "And we have homework to catch up on, and…"

Roger laughed. "Okay. I get the picture. I'll see–Oh, the president just strolled in. I guess I'd better go. I'll talk to you later. I love you."

"Love you too, Dad."

I ended the call just as Mr. Todd strolled into the Solarium. He was scarier than our parents' manager, Buddy T.

Chief of Staff

Mr. Todd looked a little rumpled, as if he had slept in his suit. He gave us a phony-looking smile.

"How are you kids doing?"

He squinted at the sunlight pouring through the windows the way a mole might do if it surfaced during the day.

"We're fine," Angela said cautiously.

P.K. said nothing.

"I love this room," Mr. Todd said. "It's so…inviting. What have you been doing?"

I nodded at the empty plates on the table. "Eating breakfast."

"I see that. I hope it was good."

"It was perfection," I said.

"Good… That's great…" He looked at P.K. "I was wondering, Willingham, if I might have a word alone with these two?"

"Their names are not 'these two,'" P.K. said. "They're Angela and Q. And you know I don't like to be called

Willingham."

"I'm sorry," Mr. Todd said. "But could I have a word with them?"

"I can't imagine what you would have to say to us that P.K. couldn't hear," Angela said sweetly. "Please stay, P.K."

Mr. Todd turned a shade redder. He obviously wasn't used to having his suggestions, which were actually orders, disobeyed.

"Very well," he said, trying to find the same horrible smile he had come in with, but failing. "I'm still curious about how you managed to get a private interview with the president."

"We contacted him before we got here this morning."

"That's interesting," Mr. Todd said. "Because I just checked all the phone and e-mail logs for the past twenty-four hours, and there is no record of you contacting the White House."

Uh-oh.

"We didn't contact the White House," Angela said without missing a beat. "We asked a friend to contact him."

"There is no record of a friend contacting him either," Mr. Todd said.

"Maybe you don't know all of his friends," I said.

"I've known John Robert Culpepper for more than twenty years. I know all of his friends. But we'll let that go for now. What did you talk about in the Oval Office?"

"He just welcomed us to the White House," Angela said. "Then he said that we should spend some time in the Oval Office by ourselves to get a feel for what it was like. It was very generous of him."

"Indeed," Mr. Todd said. "And were you alone with the

president in the Oval Office?"

Former lawyer, I thought. He was cross-examining us.

"As far as I know," Angela said. "Unless there was someone hiding under the desk."

Mr. Todd was not amused.

P.K. wasn't either, but for an entirely different reason.

"Does my dad know you're here, bullying his guests?"

"I'm not bullying anyone," Mr. Todd said. "And I'm sure he knows where I am. You can't get up to the Residence without clearance from the Secret Service."

"Right," P.K. said, sounding a little like a lawyer himself. "But once you get past duty agents they have no idea of where you are because they aren't allowed up here unless there's a credible threat."

"Good point, P.K." Agent Norton was standing in the doorway.

"Hi, Charlie," P.K. said.

Agent Norton nodded, then looked at the now-furious White House chief of staff. "So, do we have a credible threat, Mr. Todd?"

"No," Mr. Todd said quietly.

"Good. Now, if you would be so kind as to come with me, sir, I will escort you out of the Residence."

"We were just having a conversation," Mr. Todd said.

"I heard most of the exchange, and it sounded more like a grilling than a conversation. Or as P.K. put it, bullying."

"Does the president know you're up here, Agent Norton?" Mr. Todd asked.

"As a matter of fact he does. I radioed in as soon as I was

informed you were up here. He said… Well, I can't tell you exactly what he said because there are young people present. Let's just say that he was very emphatic about you vacating the Residence immediately." Norton stood to the side and swept his hand through the doorway. "After you, Mr. Todd."

The chief of staff brushed past him and said, "Perhaps you'd like to join Agent Callaghan across the street."

"Give it your best shot," Agent Norton responded, and followed him out.

I looked at P.K. for an explanation. He shrugged as if he didn't know what they were talking about either.

X-change

The little balloon text messaging on the iPhone was way cooler than the BlackBerry, although X-Ray gave me some grief about my first suspected mole.

CHECK HIM OUT!

OK. Quit yelling!

Jeez, I thought. You'd think Todd was X-Ray's uncle or something.

Before we went downstairs, P.K. filled us in on some of the security inside the White House.

In two words: armed fortress.

The countersniper team was stationed on the roof and on the grounds with shotguns, rifles, machine guns, and missile launchers, scanning the skies and the streets 24-7 for potential threats. Inside surveillance cameras covered every square inch of the house.

"If you pick your nose, someone's going to see it," P.K. said, looking at me.

"I think you should be looking at Angela," I said.

"Hilarious, Q," Angela said.

"What I mean," P.K. said, "is that when we go downstairs we're not alone, even when it looks like we're alone, except for the Oval Office, the Situation Room, and a few other offices."

"Like Mr. Todd's?" I asked.

"Right. They wouldn't have a camera in there."

"If there are no cameras up here," Angela said, "how did Mr. Todd know we were having breakfast in the Solarium?"

"One of the Residence staff tipped him off, or he

intercepted Maurice on his way back to the kitchen and asked him where we were."

So, Mr. Todd had his own mouldwarps working for him. My phone chimed.

> Todd not mole.

> You sure?

> Positive. Mountain out of molehill.

"Who are you texting?" P.K. asked.

"A friend in California."

> We're running "everyone" inside WH, but we need to narrow it down, or it will take a million years.

> We'll get you more names.

> B is on his way over to the E. Room to help set up for the concert. Most of the roadies were denied WH access because of security concerns. One of them was taken into custody because of an outstanding warrant. He's in jail.

Ouch.

Buddy T. ballistic.

I wondered how Buddy T. and Mr. Todd were going to get along.

Secret Passage

I put away the iPhone.

"Tell us about the secret passage," I said to P.K.

"It would be easier to show you."

Angela and I followed P.K. down to his bedroom. He locked the door behind us and closed the curtains.

"I found the passage a couple of years ago."

He led us into his large closet filled with clothes and turned on the light.

"It was an accident," he said. "I started keeping a diary, and I wanted to find a good place to hide it. The housecleaners come in here a couple of times a day. They wouldn't take anything, but if they found a diary I don't think they could resist peeking inside."

"Why didn't you keep the diary on your computer and password protect it?" I asked. There was a nice laptop on the desk across from his bed.

"What would be the fun of that? If you're going to keep a diary I think you should use good ink on nice paper. Did you know we have a calligraphy staff?"

"No."

"Several people full time. They've worked here for years. They create invitations, certificates, placards, citations—things like that. They're probably going crazy right now trying to get the invitations out for your parents' concert. Anyway, they've been teaching me calligraphy for three years now, and that's why I write by hand in a journal. But I needed a place to hide it." P.K. spread a row of hanging clothes. Behind it was a large white panel. "I found this." He tapped on it. "Hollow."

He put his thumbs on the top corners and pushed. The panel slid down without a sound. The dark opening was big enough for an adult to climb through.

"Wow!" Angela said.

"Yeah," P.K. said. "I was pretty surprised too when it opened like that. Inside there's a pulley system with counterbalanced weights made out of stone. I've found three passages. This one goes down to the Red Room, where Norton had you wait this morning. On the other side of the room is another panel with a passage that leads down to the Map Room, on the ground floor. The third passage is from the State Dining Room down to the housekeeper's office on the ground floor. I think there's another passage from the East Room down to the Library, but I haven't found it yet."

"How'd you find these passages?" Angela asked.

"School," P.K. answered. "If there was one passage, I figured there were more. I did a project on White House architecture and renovation. There're advantages and disadvantages to being the President's Kid. One advantage is that I can talk to anyone about anything. Bethany contacted a guy at the National Archives who knows more about the White House than anyone on earth."

"Except maybe you," Angela said.

"Maybe," P.K. said, flushing a little. "He didn't know about the passages...at least he didn't say anything to me about them. And I didn't tell him what I was really doing there. We spent the day looking at old architectural drawings, and I was able to figure out where the other passages might be. It took me a year to find them."

I stuck my head through the opening and saw a small green light blinking. It was attached to a radio charger. I came back out with the radio.

"I see you did a little electrical work inside too," I said.

"Yeah," P.K. said. "I couldn't very well charge the radio in plain sight on my desk."

He was full of surprises.

Angela took the radio. "Where'd you get this?"

"It's an old one. The Secret Service upgraded to a new model at the beginning of the year. I took one out of the box they dumped the old ones into. I couldn't help it. It was just sitting on the floor out in the open in W-16."

"What's W-16?" I asked.

"It's a room below the Oval Office where agents hang out when they're off duty."

"The signals are encrypted and changed every day," Angela said. "How do you get the codes?"

"Sometimes several times a day," P.K. said. "How do you know that?"

Angela bit her lower lip as she always did just before she spilled her guts. In the past I had stepped in and stopped her, but I let it go this time. P.K. knew something was up, and if we didn't give him something he was just going to get more suspicious.

"My mother was a Secret Service agent," she said. "When I was little she was assigned to the White House for a while."

"She's obviously not Blaze Tucker," P.K. said. "Where's your real mom now?"

"She was killed in the line of duty," Angela answered.

"I'm sorry," P.K. said, and looked it. "I lost my mom too."

"I know," Angela said, handing the radio to him.

"Did my dad know your mom?" P.K. asked quietly.

Angela nodded. "I think that's why he really invited us to the Oval Office this morning."

She was telling the truth…kind of.

"I can see that," P.K. said. "Dad has a soft spot for agents."

"So, how do you get the codes?" Angela asked.

"I don't always get them," P.K. answered. "Sometimes I think adults think kids are deaf or don't understand English. If I'm there at the right time, I pick up the codes when I'm in W-16. Or I borrow a radio from one of the agents to talk to another agent. I guess they don't think we can read either."

Most ten-year-old kids weren't Willingham Culpepper.

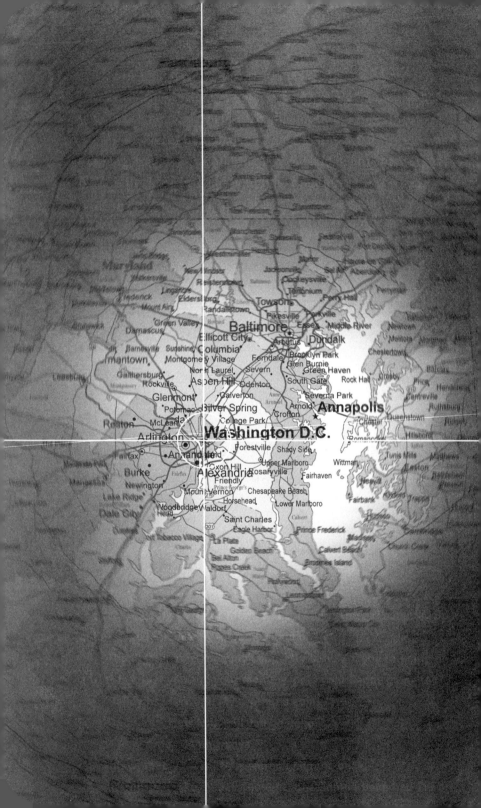

SATURDAY, SEPTEMBER 6 >

10:37 a.m. to 1:30 p.m.

Tour

Agent Norton was waiting for us at the bottom of the stairs leading up to the Residence. I thought he might be friendlier after the Solarium encounter with Mr. Todd, but he had the same neutral Secret *Serious* expression from a few hours before. Maybe he was annoyed at having to follow a bunch of kids around, or maybe he was worried about joining Agent Callaghan across the street. Whoever Agent Callaghan was. Whatever the reason, he fell in a discreet thirty feet behind and dogged us like Croc, stopping when we stopped and walking when we walked.

P.K. was right. A lot of people worked in the White House, and he seemed to know most of them by their first and last names. This would have been helpful to us if any of them acted like moles, but none of them did. From the calligraphers to the florists to the carpenters, they acted like normal people busily getting ready for the last-minute concert they weren't invited to.

I asked P.K. about who was going to the concert.

"My sister's friends, senators, members of Congress, their families, a few staffers from the East and West wings, the vice president and his family, generals, admirals, cabinet members, lobbyists..."

"Any White House staff?"

"Just people working the event. Secret Service Uniformed Division and plainclothes, waitstaff, ushers..."

"But not the florists, carpenters, cooks, or housekeeping staff?"

"They're not in Bethany and Dad's social circle," P.K. said. "I'm not saying Dad and Bethany are stuck-up or snotty— Dad would rather hang out with Chef Cheesy than his chief of staff—but the concert and the brunch are really political events, not social events. Besides, the concert's being held in the East Room. It's not big enough to hold everyone who works here."

"How about fifty of them?" Angela chimed in, knowing exactly what I was getting at.

Roger and Mom had insisted on keeping their regular concert ticket prices low (much to Buddy T.'s annoyance). Sharing their music was more important to them than money. They would rather sing and play for twice as many people than charge twice as much for tickets. One of Mom's favorite sayings was, "Do what you love and the money will follow." I wasn't sure if this was going to hold true for me and Angela. I wanted to become a professional magician. Angela wanted to become a federal agent.

"They could probably squeeze in fifty more people," P.K. said. "But Bethany will probably freak out." He grinned. "Which might be kind of fun."

I pulled out my phone…

> Only VIPs invited to your concert. I think we should invite 50 WH people who work to put this together. Angela and I and First Son (P.K.) would like to pick them.

> Let me check with Roger and B.C.

I showed the screen to P.K. and Angela.

"Right now Bethany has a frozen smile on her face," P.K. said. "Inside she's having a coronary."

The discussion, or heart attack, lasted about ten minutes.

> 30 people including family members. Bethany's social secretary is on the way to see you.

I guess everything was a negotiation and compromise in D.C.

> Great! Thanks, Mom.

> Brunch is about to begin. Are you sure you don't want to join us?

We had been carefully avoiding the dining room where the brunch was being held so we wouldn't get sucked in for several hours.

> No thanks. We're good.

> I'm sure. Love you.

The social secretary hurried down the hall toward us. I guess when the First Daughter spoke you moved–quickly. He was dressed in an expensive-looking suit, starched salmon-colored shirt, pink tie, and matching handkerchief. He was carrying a brown leather briefcase.

"You must be Will!" he said breathlessly.

This was the first person we had met who didn't know P.K.

"My name is Wayne Arbuckle. I presume you're Angie and Quest?"

"Angela," Angela said.

"Q," I said.

"P.K.," P.K. said.

"Of course."

"How long have you worked here?" P.K. asked.

"Seven months." He looked at Angela and me. "I hear you had some excitement early this morning."

We looked at him blankly. I didn't know what Angela was thinking, but I was wondering how he had heard about Agent Norton tossing Mr. Todd out of the Solarium. I was wrong.

"Meeting with the president?" Arbuckle said. "Unusual

timing, but what an honor for both of you. What was it like?"

"Brief," I said.

"What did you talk about?"

"He just welcomed us to the White House," Angela said.

"Well, as you might imagine, it's the talk of the house this morning."

Interestingly, Arbuckle was the first person we'd met who had mentioned it, although I was sure he was right. The staff had to be talking about it.

Arbuckle looked at P.K. "Will your father be attending the concert?"

P.K. shrugged. "I don't know."

"The reason I ask," Arbuckle said, "is we're all a little perplexed this morning. He's canceled all of his appointments and hasn't let us know why or what he plans to do instead. Even the Secret Service doesn't know his revised schedule."

I glanced at Angela. She gave me an imperceptible nod. I pulled my phone out.

"A friend just texted me," I said. It was a lie. I texted X-Ray.

> Wayne Arbuckle. Bethany Culpepper's social secretary.

> Got it.

Arbuckle reached into his briefcase and came out with a stack of cards embossed with the presidential seal in gold. He handed them to P.K.

"These just came from the engraver. The invitations are all printed up except for the names of the invitees. The calligraphy office asked if you could do the honor of filling out the names as you give them to people. They're really under the gun right now."

"Sure, but I don't have my–"

Arbuckle produced an ink bottle and calligraphy pen. "They said you might need these."

"Thanks."

I took the pen and ink and put them into one of my pockets. Angela took the cards and stuffed them into her pack.

"You're going to make a lot of people happy today," Arbuckle said. "And jealous. The First Daughter said no infants or toddlers, and everyone, regardless of age, must have a personalized invitation to gain entrance. All I ask is that you give me a list of the invitees so I can pass the names along to the Secret Service." He reached inside his jacket and pulled out his cell phone. "In fact, Q, if you could give me your cell phone number, I'll call you later and you can read me the list of names over the phone. That way you won't forget."

I didn't know my cell number. I started to pull the phone out of my pocket.

"That's okay," Angela said. "We won't forget. Do you have a card with your phone number and e-mail?"

Angela was right–again. We weren't supposed to give out our number or e-mail addresses. And for a split second I saw *something* in Arbuckle's face. A look. Like a mask slipping, but he pushed it back up so fast I wasn't sure I saw what I thought I saw. I'm pretty good at reading people–a skill all good magicians have—but whatever I'd seen was gone. *Poof!*

Smiling pleasantly, Arbuckle reached into his pocket and pulled out a business card, which he handed to Angela.

"We'll get you the list," she said, putting the card in her pack.

Malak slept late.

When she woke she found a travel mug of black coffee on the table next to the bed with a note: "Breakfast upstairs."

The coffee and the note disturbed her.

Badly.

They meant that someone had come into her room and she had not woken.

Leopards caught sleeping die.

Malak took her coffee outside onto the patio.

Blue sky. A chill was in the air. A beautiful day, but no one would remember the weather after the sun set. Amun had told her the night before that today would be a day that no one in the United States would forget, but had given her no specifics about the terrible thing that would happen or where.

"Hi."

Malak turned quickly. It was the little girl. For the second time that morning someone had stepped into her space without her being aware, and this time she was awake. What's happening to me? she thought.

"Good morning," Malak said to the girl, masking her confusion.

"The trees are beautiful."

The girl nodded. "The leaves are turning golden."

"What are you doing today?" Malak asked.

"We're going on a trip. Mommy's packing." The girl squinted up at her. "You look like my mommy...kind of."

"Thank you. Your mommy's a pretty lady. So, you're going on a trip? Is it just you and your mommy, or is your daddy going too?"

"Daddy has to work. My brother's going."

"Of course. How long will you be gone?"

"A long time, Mommy says."

This probably meant they weren't coming back.

Another mistake, Malak thought. She should have had Ziv or Dirk follow the little girl's father to wherever he worked. There was more to his assignment than picking her up from the train station. Pulling an established, well-positioned asset from a safe house could mean only one thing: Daddy was going to do something very bad.

"Are you driving or flying?" Malak asked.

"Driving," the girl answered. "The big car."

Of course they would be driving. No surveillance cameras. No identification to show. No trail to follow.

Malak was about to ask some more questions when the girl's mother appeared, holding her son in her arms. She had a computer case hanging from her shoulder.

"I'm sorry," she said. "It's difficult to keep track of both of them."

Malak smiled. "That's fine. We were just talking about the leaves turning color. Are you going somewhere?"

"I have some errands to run."

The girl was about to say something, but a harsh look from

her mother silenced her. The training started young, Malak remembered. Her own parents had treated her the same way when she was growing up. So many secrets, which she never understood until now. Unlike her twin, Anmar, when Malak came of age she chose a different path. She had joined the other side. Her parents, or the man and woman whom she thought of as her parents, disowned her, and then they disappeared.

How would the girl choose when she came of age?

How would the boy choose?

"Help yourself to anything in the kitchen," the woman said.

Malak saw anxiety in the woman's brown eyes but knew better than to ask any questions.

Ghosts did not ask questions.

"Thank you," Malak said. "As sala'amu alaikum. Peace be upon you."

"She says those funny words like Daddy," the girl said.

The woman took her daughter's hand and walked around the side of the house.

Malak waited twenty seconds, then hurried through the patio door and upstairs. She looked out the window and memorized the license plate number of the late model SUV as it headed down the long driveway.

Then she began to search the house.

It was as sterile as a well-cleaned hotel room. She did not find a single scrap of paper—not even an old grocery list or receipt, and certainly nothing with the family's names on it.

Malak had seen this many times before.

The woman had loaded prepacked suitcases into the SUV, thrown the laptop into her bag, grabbed her two children, and driven away as if they had never lived in the beautiful house. Her next house might not be as nice, but it wouldn't matter to her or her husband—if he joined her. They would enroll their children in school, get jobs, and wait for instructions.

Malak retrieved her backpack from the bedroom and brought it up to the kitchen. She pulled out her computer and composed a carefully written encrypted e-mail as she ate a bowl of cereal.

The e-mail was not to her handler, Amun Massri. It was to a man who called himself Ziv. He had been with her from almost the beginning of this deception, and he was the only person in the world she trusted absolutely.

Before sending the e-mail, Malak went over it several times to make sure her instructions were crystal clear. Ziv would need Tyrone Boone's help to carry them out.

Invitations

By the time P.K., Angela, Norton, and I got to the kitchen, we'd given out most of the invitations to surprised and grateful staff members.

"Kids!" Chef Conrad hurried over to us.

P.K. had been right. Conrad was small. In fact, we were all taller than the little chef, but he made up for his stature by his big personality.

"Why are you not at the brunch?" He pointed to a flat-screen television monitor hanging on the wall above us. It was a live video feed of the brunch. Mom and Roger were sitting at the head of a long table, chatting with the people.

"Because it would be totally boring," P.K. said.

"Or perhaps it is because your friends do not like my food." Chef Conrad pointed his finger at me. "You did not eat my cheese curds and vanilla milkshake."

"I fell asleep," I said.

"Who falls asleep in the presence of deep-fried perfection?"

"Sorry," I said.

Conrad smiled. "I will make you an order of my fried cheese curds right now."

"We just ate breakfast," I said.

"Your sister had no problem finishing her cheese curds and hamburger," Conrad said. "When they retrieved her plates this morning, housekeeping thought they had been washed."

I looked at Angela the vegetarian.

"The cheese curds were unbelievable," Angela said. "I was hungry after our meeting."

"With the great man!" Conrad said. "And so early in the morning too. Nice of the president to find time for you."

"It was," Angela said. "We were wondering if you wanted to go to the Match concert."

"That's very kind of you, but I'll be working tonight. The First Daughter has requested that hors d'oeuvres be served before your parents' performance. We will prepare them here, stage them up in the State Dining Room, and then wheel them down the hall to the East Room."

"When do you sleep?" I asked.

Conrad leaned toward us conspiratorially and whispered, "Sometimes I sleep in the kitchen unless someone orders fried cheese curds, milkshakes, and hamburgers before dawn."

We laughed.

"Seriously," he continued. "I'll go home after the brunch, sleep for a few hours, and then come back to help make the hors d'oeuvres."

"Do you always use surveillance cameras on your diners?" Angela asked.

"Not up in the Residence," Conrad answered. "But for big

events like this and the concert tonight it allows us to keep track of how the food is holding up. And of course, I like to see if our guests are enjoying my food. Are you spending another night here?"

"I don't know," Angela said, and looked at me.

I shrugged. I hadn't heard anything about spending a second night.

"When I return," Conrad said. "I will make all of you a plate of fried cheese curds."

We left so he could get back to monitoring the brunch.

Agent Norton hadn't said a word to us since we'd started our tour, but that changed when we left the kitchen and walked up to the first floor.

"Can I talk to you a second?" he said.

"Sure," we said in unison.

"Let's step into this room," he said.

The room was the same place we had waited the night before for POTUS–the same room with the secret passage. Agent Norton closed the door behind us. I looked at P.K. and Angela. They looked like I felt–worried. Had Agent Norton seen something earlier that morning?

"How many of those invitations do you have left?" he asked.

Which was a lot better than: *Tell me about the secret passages. Or: What are you doing with an encrypted Secret Service radio?*

I thought P.K. might faint in relief.

"Not many," Angela said, slipping her pack off her shoulder.

"I just need one," Agent Norton said.

"Won't you be with us?" I asked.

Norton nodded. "It's not for me."

"Wife?" Angela asked. "Girlfriend?"

Agent Norton shook his head. "A friend."

"Okay," P.K. said.

Angela pulled out an invitation, and I pulled out P.K.'s ink and calligraphy pen.

P.K. sat down with the invitation. "You know your friend will have to get through security."

Agent Norton smiled. "Yes, I knew that. Don't worry. This guy will make it through. His name is Patrick James Callaghan."

It took me a couple of seconds to remember where I'd heard the name. "The guy across the street?"

"You don't miss much," Agent Norton said.

"I try not to. Who is he?"

"A big fan of your parents."

"What's he doing across the street?" Angela asked.

"He works there."

P.K. finished the invitation and handed it to Norton.

"Thanks," Agent Norton said. "He'll be happy." He put the invitation inside his suit pocket. "Where to next?"

"The Rose Garden," P.K. said. "Then the Press Briefing Room."

"Not the briefing room," Agent Norton said.

"What's a tour without the briefing room?" P.K. said.

Agent Norton shook his head. "Where's my hazmat suit?"

P.K and Angela laughed.

I didn't get it.

"Hazardous material suit," Angela translated.

It turned out that Angela didn't get it either. She thought Agent Norton was making a joke about the sometimes "toxic" relationship between the president and the press. What he was referring to was the mess inside and outside the press, or briefing, room.

The White House is immaculately clean. The Press Briefing Room, and the path leading up to it, is a dump. Cigarette butts, squished gum, candy wrappers, Styrofoam coffee cups (some with floating butts) were strewn all over the place.

"What's this?" I asked.

"A war of wills," P.K. answered. "Dad doesn't believe that taxpayers should subsidize picking up after people who refuse to pick up after themselves. Every few months Bethany tries to negotiate a truce by sending in a housekeeping force to clean things up. This is followed by a plea for the press to stop being slobs. They usually honor the accord for about three days, and then it's back to garbage as usual. Looks like Bethany needs to broker another deal."

Agent Norton peeked through the briefing room door, then walked back to us.

"They're having a press conference," he said. "I wouldn't recommend going in right now unless you want to be swarmed."

"Is the president doing the briefing?" Angela asked.

Norton shook his head. "The sweaty press secretary is fielding questions, trying to explain why the president inexplicably canceled all of his appointments. Of course the secretary has no idea why, which is why he's sweating." He looked at P.K. "Do you know why?"

P.K. shrugged. "I haven't seen Dad in two days."

I wondered what it would be like not seeing your dad for a couple of days while you're living under the same roof.

"Maybe we should just head over to the Rose Garden," Norton suggested.

"Might as well," P.K. agreed.

We started in that direction, but we were stopped by a familiar voice behind us.

"Angela! Q!"

Shocked, we turned around. It was Dirk Peski–short, unshaved, unsavory as usual, with two digital cameras hanging around his thick neck.

"How'd you get in here?" Angela asked.

Dirk held up a laminated ID on a lanyard tangled with his camera straps. "Member of the press," he said.

"I hardly think being a freelance tabloid photographer qualifies you for White House press credentials," Angela said.

I elbowed her in the side. Norton looked like he was about to draw his gun and shoot him. Dirk was oblivious to the potential threat. He did work for the tabloids and was known as the Paparazzi Prince. Our first encounter with him had been in Grand Island, Nebraska, where he had tracked us down and caused a minor riot and blackmailed Boone into letting him have an exclusive interview with our parents. Our second encounter had been in Philadelphia, where we found out that Dirk was using his obnoxious paparazzi persona as a cover. He actually worked for Malak. Or as his partner, Ziv, told us: "I'm the monkey that watches the leopard's tail. I'm her second pair of eyes and ears. I make certain that no one stalks her while she stalks her prey. But she's a good leopard. She only kills those who deserve to die." I assumed this job description applied to Dirk as well, although he looked more like a chimp than a monkey.

"I'm just kidding, Dirk," Angela said, getting my not-so-subtle hint. "It's great to see you! Dad and Blaze will be thrilled you're here."

Nothing could be further from the truth, but Roger and Mom had no idea who Dirk really was or what was going on. And we couldn't tell them. If they found out they would very likely give up everything they had worked so hard for.

"Yeah," Dirk said. "I wanted to surprise them."

Sickened would be more like it, I thought.

"This is Will," Angela said, "President Culpepper's son. And this is Agent Norton."

"Nice meeting you," Dirk said, barely giving either of them a glance. "I need to talk to you kids alone."

"What for?" Norton asked.

"For about two minutes," Dirk said. "*Private* family business."

"It's okay," I said.

Norton stared at me for a second, then gave a curt nod. "Stand where I can see you." He looked at Dirk. "Hand your cameras over."

"Sure thing," Dirk said, giving him the cameras. "If you take any good shots, let me know and I'll e-mail them to you."

Norton did not smile.

We walked about fifty feet away before Dirk stopped.

"What's going on?" Angela asked.

"I need one of those invitations."

"How do you know about the invitations?" I asked.

"Boone."

"When did you talk to him?" Angela asked.

"We don't have time for this," Dirk said. "Mr. S.S. is giving us the stink eye."

I glanced back. He was right. Norton was staring at us.

"And the deal is," Dirk continued, "you need to give the invitation to me without him seeing."

That was going to be a trick, with the invitations inside Angela's bag.

"We'll have to ask Boone," Angela said.

"Go ahead," Dirk said. "But make it quick."

> Dirk is at the WH. He wants an invitation to the concert.

> Give it to him. I'm in the East Room, setting up. Swing by.

I showed the screen to Angela.

"How are we going to get Will to fill it out?" Angela asked. "The invitations are supposed to be for staff members. He was a little uncomfortable filling out an invitation for Agent Norton."

"He asked for an invitation?" Dirk asked.

"For a friend of his," I said.

"Who?"

"A guy named Patrick James Callaghan."

Dirk seemed to make a mental note of this, then said, "Keep the invitation blank. I'll fill it in later."

Dirk didn't look like he was capable of counterfeiting P.K.'s calligraphy, but that was his problem. My problem was trying to figure out how to slip him an invitation without the hawk-eyed Norton seeing it.

"We'll still need a name," Angela said. "We have to send a list to the social secretary. They'll be checking the invitation against the list at the gate."

"Warren Parker," Dirk said.

"Who's that?" Angela asked.

"No one you'd recognize."

"I'll handle the invitation," I said to Angela. "Give me your pack."

I palmed a deck of cards from my pocket as she set the pack down and opened it.

"Want to see a new card trick?" I asked Dirk.

"What?"

"Just play along," I whispered.

"Sure," Dirk said too loudly. "I'd love to see a new trick."

I reached inside the pack and pulled out an invitation, but made it look like I was fishing out the deck of cards. I handed the deck to Dirk. "Look them over to make sure it's an ordinary deck."

Dirk gave the cards a cursory look. "Yeah, they look normal."

"Mix them up," I said.

Magicians always have to be ready for the unexpected. As

Dirk was mixing the cards, P.K. started over to see the trick, followed by Agent Norton.

"Nice going, Slick," Dirk whispered.

"The trick's over," I whispered back.

"What do you—"

P.K. reached us. Agent Norton stood about ten feet behind him.

"Okay," I said. "I want you to memorize three cards. Can you do that?"

"Of course I can do that," Dirk said.

"Mix the cards up again really well."

He mixed them.

"Give me the *entire* deck."

He passed me the deck.

I looked at P.K. "Can you give me a hand?"

"Sure."

"I mean literally. Hold out your hand."

I started counting out the cards. "One…two…," until I got to the last card, "…forty-nine." I looked at Dirk. "I asked for the entire deck."

"I gave you the entire deck," Dirk said.

I shook my head. "It's three cards short. You're holding out on me."

Dirk held up his pudgy hands. "I gave you what you gave me."

This is where it got tricky, because I was no longer in control of the real trick.

"There are three cards in the right pocket of your suit jacket."

"No there aren't," Dirk said.

"Yes there are," I said. "But before you pull them out tell me the three cards you chose."

"Three of diamonds, five of hearts, ace of spades."

"Good. Reach into your pocket...*slowly.*" I didn't usually add slowly to the trick, but I wanted to give Dirk a chance to figure out what the real trick really was.

He reached into his pocket and started feeling around, and then he smiled. "That's pretty good, Q." He carefully pulled out the three cards leaving the blank invitation in his pocket. "You should have an act in Vegas."

"Maybe I will someday. Hold up the cards."

The cards were the three of diamonds, five of hearts, and ace of spades.

"How'd you do that?" P.K. asked.

"Yeah," Dirk echoed. "How *did* you do that?"

Agent Norton didn't seem to care. He handed Dirk his cameras.

"Magic," I said.

The East Room

Halfway to the East Room we were intercepted by another Secret Service agent. It was the same woman who had greeted us at the gate the night before.

Norton looked at his watch, which just happened to be an Omega Seamaster exactly like ours. Apparently, Malak wasn't the only agent to do J.R. a big favor. Either that or Norton just liked the watch.

"Time for me to get some shut-eye," he said. "This is Agent Call. She'll be with you until after dinner. I'll be back to take you to the concert. How many invitations do you have left?"

"I'm not sure," Angela said. "Not many. Do you need another one?"

"No," Norton answered. "I just want to make sure that when you give the last one out you e-mail the list to Wayne Arbuckle. Otherwise, the people you invited won't be able to get through the gate."

"Nice watch," I said. Norton had to have noticed that Angela and I were wearing the same watch he and the president wore when we left the Oval Office. Why hadn't he said anything?

"You've got good taste," Norton said, and walked away.

Agent Call was friendlier and more polished than Norton, which turned out to be a little annoying. It meant that she gave us three feet instead of ten and rattled on like a White House tour guide.

"Abigail Adams hung her laundry in here to dry," she explained as we walked into the East Room. "It's the biggest room in the White House."

It was filled with people cleaning, setting up chairs and tables, spreading tablecloths, and filling vases with beautiful flowers. No one was hanging laundry. Boone was standing on a small stage on the opposite side of the room, helping the roadies set up equipment. Buddy T. was next to him, saying something that Boone seemed to be totally ignoring. We walked over to them.

Boone smiled.

Buddy T. scowled. I never thought he liked us very much. He had tried to talk our parents out of having us come along on the tour.

"How y'all doin'?" Boone said.

The good ol' boy dropping the "g" was fake. Boone used it only when he was playing the ancient roadie, which was most of the time.

"We're fine," Angela said. "Boone, this is the president's son, Will. And this is Agent Call."

"Pleasure to meet both of you," Boone said, shaking their hands.

"And this is Buddy T.," Angela continued. "Our parents' manager."

"I can't believe that you only let three of my roadies in," Buddy T. complained to Agent Call, ignoring P.K. "How do you expect me to set up a command performance with three guys?"

"Security is tight at the White House," Agent Call explained calmly. "I don't know the details, but when they ran your people through our database, red flags must have come up. Sorry."

"Because of you they're out partying in D.C. on my dime," Buddy T. said. "And we're doing this concert for free."

It was actually our parents' dime. Our parents paid for everything, including Buddy T.'s salary. And they were performing for free, but the publicity they were getting by playing the White House would more than make up for the loss.

Buddy T. was about to say more, but we were saved by the bell, or the song. His cell phone sounded with our parents' number one hit, "Rekindled." He walked away, yelling at the person on the other end.

"Hey, Teddy?" Boone called to one of the other roadies. "Why don't you give Will a tour of how all this equipment works?"

A young guy with long brown hair came over. "Sure thing, Boone."

"Will's the president's son," Boone said.

"You can call me P.K."

"President's Kid?" Teddy said.

"Yeah."

"Cool. Follow me, P.K., and I'll show you how we make musicians sound better than they really are."

"In your dreams, Ted," Boone said. "I'll take Q and Angela with me to get the last load of equipment."

Agent Call looked a little confused for a moment, then followed Teddy and P.K., which I think is exactly what Boone had in mind. He wanted to talk to us alone and knew that Agent Call would stick with P.K. Divide and conquer.

He led us out to the semi carrying Match's concert equipment. There were actually two trucks for the tour. The second one was on its way to the next gig. The semis would be hopscotching their way across the country for the next year. The truck was surrounded by half a dozen uniformed Secret Service agents and a couple of bomb-sniffing dogs.

Angela and I climbed into the back of the truck first. As Boone followed, his shirt cuff hiked up and I noticed that he was wearing an Omega Seamaster on his wrist. It was the first time I'd seen him wearing a watch. He saw me staring at it and held it up so I could see it better. From the scratches on the band and bezel it looked like he'd had it for a long time.

"I don't know how many people J.R. has given these to," he said. "But it's a very exclusive club. It means he trusts you, and you can trust him. I was just as surprised as you were when he gave you yours. I haven't worn mine in years, but thought I should slip it on in case I run into Malak again. I want her to know I can be trusted."

I think she already knew that. When we saw her in Philly she charged Boone and the SOS team with protecting her only daughter with their lives.

"Agent Norton has a Seamaster too," Angela said.

Boone took off his watch and flipped it over. "He might just like the brand." On the underside was another crystal showing the intricate mechanical movement inside the watch. Etched into the sapphire glass were ten tiny numbers: 8633726837.

Angela and I took our Seamasters off and looked. They had the same numbers.

"That used to be J.R.'s private landline, but he had it transferred over to his private cell number," Boone said. "The only other agent I know, aside from me and Malak, who has one like ours is a guy named Pat Callaghan."

"Agent Norton asked P.K. for an invitation for Patrick Callaghan!" Angela said.

"That's interesting," Boone said. "Maybe Norton's in J.R.'s club after all."

"Who's Pat Callaghan?" I asked.

"Right now he's an undercover protester camped across the street in Lafayette Park."

"You're kidding."

Boone shook his head. "Let's hope he's home getting cleaned up for the concert. Personal invitation or not, there's no way they'd let him in looking the way he did early this morning when I talked to him."

"Why would he volunteer for that duty?" Angela asked.

"He didn't volunteer. He got booted out for some infraction, and the Secret Service has thousands of those."

"But he has the watch," I said.

"J.R. probably doesn't even know he's across the street.

And Pat would never tell him. That's part of the code: Thou shalt not whine to the president of the United States. Pat's always been a little bit of a rogue. He makes up his own rules in order to get results. Kind of like your mom," he said, looking at Angela. "Pat knows something's up, and like all good agents, he knows more than he's saying. Norton does too. I don't know Norton, but it will be good to have Pat in the room. How many invitations do you have left?"

"One," Angela answered.

"Give it to me. I want as many of our people in the East Room tonight as we can get. Do you know if J.R. is going to be at the concert?"

I shook my head. "Even P.K. doesn't know."

"J.R. won't make up his mind until the very last second. He just sent everyone scrambling by announcing that he wanted to go golfing. The motorcade just pulled out, but I wouldn't be surprised if halfway there he tells his detail he's changed his mind and wants to go to see the Washington Nationals play the New York Mets."

Angela handed Boone the last invitation. "You'll have to fill it out yourself. Who's it for?"

"Vanessa."

Vanessa was the SOS team's official driver. She was in her seventies. Aside from being a professional driver, she was very good with a throwing knife.

I was keeping the list on my iPhone. I pulled it out. "I'll need her last name."

"Orbit," Boone said.

I added her name, then copied the list and pasted it into

an e-mail to Wayne Arbuckle. "I'm curious," I said. "When I send this list to the social secretary, will he have my e-mail address?"

Boone shook his head. "Not exactly. If he e-mails you back, it will go to a server inside the intellimobile, where X-Ray will screen it. If he wants you to reply, he'll forward it to you."

"So our e-mail is screened?" Angela asked.

"Everyone on the SOS team's e-mail is screened, including mine," Boone answered. "No secrets, at least among us."

"No privacy," I added.

"That too," Boone said.

"How did Arbuckle check out?" I asked.

"He looks legit. No red flags. All the other names you sent checked out too, but that doesn't mean much. Before anyone gets a job inside the White House, the FBI and Secret Service do thorough background checks. The mole or moles we're trying to dig up will all have impeccable credentials. X-Ray is running backgrounds on everyone inside, but so far nothing has come up, which means we have to keep an eye on everyone."

"Who's Warren Parker?" I asked, sending the e-mail.

"Is that the name Dirk gave you?"

I nodded.

"I suspect that's Ziv," Boone answered. "Warren Parker isn't his real name of course, nor is Ziv, for that matter. I met him at Starbucks this morning. He filled me in on what's going on. When I told him about the invitations, he said he'd try to get Dirk inside to get one from you."

"So, what is going on?" Angela asked.

"Your mother spent last night in a safe house in McLean, Virginia, with a young couple and their two small children. When she got up this morning the mother packed the SUV with the family's clothes and the two kids, and took off. The husband had already left. They're not coming back, which means they're going to do something bad. Malak wanted us to find the mother and follow her. X-Ray managed to find the SUV–don't ask me how–and Eben and another SOS guy, Everett, got on her tail. She went to Dulles Airport. In the short-term parking garage she turned the kids over to another woman, and they headed into the terminal. Everett followed the kids. Eben followed the mom in her SUV. The only problem was that the mother wasn't in the SUV. It was being driven by another woman who managed to ditch Eben at the Tysons Corner mall. She went into a lingerie shop. If Eben followed her in, he'd stick out like an athletic cup, so he waited outside. She never came out. The SUV is still in the parking lot. There is not one shot of her on any of the mall surveillance cameras, though there are several shots of Eben looking like he's going to go postal after he lost her."

I'd seen that look on Eben's face up close and personal. It wasn't pleasant.

"Everett didn't fare much better," Boone said. "The woman and the kids had boarding passes when they walked into the airport, and carry-on bags. They went directly to the TSA security line. Everett couldn't follow them through without a ticket. It took him fifteen minutes to get one. In that time fifty-seven flights took off. The woman and the kids were gone. X-Ray is checking all the airline manifests for a woman and two kids for that time period, but so far he's coming up empty. She probably got past TSA and handed the kids off to other people. She might have even split them up. Not counting the two kids, that's a minimum of three people in the ghost cell operating here in D.C. Four, if you count Malak. Five, if you count Amun Massri, who paid a visit to Malak last night at the safe house. That's a lot of terrorist ghosts floating around town."

I knew that Amun Massri was the guy who'd set the bomb at Independence Hall that killed Malak's twin sister. According to Malak, Amun was the key to finding out who was running the ghost cell.

"What did Amun want with Malak?" Angela asked.

"Ziv didn't say, and I'm not sure he knows. What I do know is that the ghost cell is made up of the best operatives I've ever seen. Wherever they go they assume they're being followed by well-trained professionals."

"Maybe they knew they were being followed," I said.

Boone shook his head. "Eben and Everett are pros. But they got bested today."

"What else did Ziv say?" Angela asked.

"He said to say hello to you two." Boone smiled. "By the way, what did he look like when you talked to him at Independence Park?"

"He looked like a Philadelphia cop," I said.

"Midfifties," Angela added. "Blue eyes, a little overweight, slight accent, bald."

"Today he had brown hair, brown eyes, mustache, glasses, and was dressed in a nice business suit with a pistol underneath his jacket. That will probably be the Warren Parker you see tonight, minus the pistol. If something goes down at the concert we'll have Vanessa, me, Ziv, Marie, Art, and maybe Pat Callaghan, although I don't know what Pat is up to yet."

Marie and Art were our parents' personal assistants, or PAs. Mom and Roger didn't know it, but they were also their bodyguards and worked for SOS. They were waiting for us when we returned to the East Room.

Marie and Art

Marie and Art were younger than the other members of SOS by at least two decades.

Marie was petite with thick black hair. Her brown eyes were clear, alert, and a bit exotic. She looked like she had some Native American blood running through her veins.

Art was just the opposite of Marie. He was tall, muscular, with curly red hair, freckles, and blue eyes. Both of them had nice smiles.

Angela and I had seen them backstage at the Electric Factory the night before in Philadelphia, but we hadn't met them formally.

"I'm Marie."

"I'm Art."

Angela and I shook their hands.

"Best PAs in the business," Buddy T. said. "Your parents are lucky I found them."

Buddy T. did not find them. Boone had told Heather Hughes, the president of the record company, to hire them.

We still hadn't figured out how Heather fit into all of this. All we knew was that she did anything Boone asked her to do, like hire the two PAs/covert operatives standing in front of us. They knew that we knew—and we knew that they knew—that Buddy T. knew nothing about why they were really there.

"Your parents are holding a press conference with the First Daughter," Marie said. "When they finish they're going up to the Solarium and would like to have you join them."

Buddy T. gave us a sour look. Well, I should say a *sourer* look.

"We weren't invited," Art said cheerfully.

"When you see 'em," Buddy T. said, "ask 'em if they might have some time to talk to their manager about a little thing called their concert tour!"

His cell phone rang. He pulled it from his belt clip and put it to his ear.

Malak walked down the path to the Potomac. It had been years since she'd been on the river. When she was stationed at the White House she was on the Secret Service sculling team. The boat tied up to the small dock was a kayak, not a scull. Nevertheless, she was looking forward to the short paddle to the Georgetown part of D.C.

As usual, Amun had thought of everything. Inside the red kayak was a lightweight wetsuit in her size, a helmet, a pair of gloves, a waterproof bag, even a water bottle. Malak stripped off her clothes, pulled on the wetsuit, then zipped her clothes into the waterproof bag along with her small pack and stowed it behind the seat.

She pushed a few feet away from the dock, found her balance and her stroke, then plunged into the main current. And for a few glorious minutes she was no longer Anmar, the Leopard, she was Malak Tucker the Secret Service agent...

Heady times. Traveling on Air Force One, protecting the most powerful man in the world with the best group of people she had ever worked with. She had three families back then—the First Family, her own family, and her Secret Service family. It was difficult to juggle all of them, but hard as it was, it was nothing compared to the tightrope she was on now.

She scanned the banks on both sides of the river. She didn't see anyone watching her, but that didn't mean they weren't there. An anonymous e-mail may have been sent, something like...

I'll meet you for a jog along the Potomac on Chain Bridge at 1 p.m. Look for a red kayak. I'll expect to hear from you.

Amun always knew where she had been and where to find her—almost always. It had taken a lot of work, but she had managed to slip his ghost watchers for a few precious minutes in Philadelphia with Ziv and Dirk's help. It had been very dangerous for all of them, but worth it—at least for her.

As Malak neared the boathouse she thought about her old sculling partners. Amanda, Pat, and Charlie. It had been difficult for them to get time off at the same time to practice. They called their four-person team the Scull and Crossbones. They even had T-shirts made with a vertical scull as the skull and two crossed sculling oars beneath as the crossbones. If they couldn't get off during the day together, they would scull on the Potomac at night.

What would my old friends think of me now, Malak thought as she paddled up to the boathouse. They would shoot me dead like an escaped leopard from the National Zoo.

With a sigh she took the waterproof bag with her pack and clothes out of the kayak. No one at the busy boathouse gave her a second look as she made her way to the restroom to change, which had been the entire reason for the kayak and wetsuit. Who would suspect a middle-aged woman in a kayak of being a notorious international terrorist?

When Malak stepped back out, wearing sunglasses and with her hair tucked under a worn Washington Nationals baseball cap, she found Amun waiting for her. She figured he had had a spotter along the Potomac. She hadn't told him when to expect her at the boathouse.

"Any problems?" he asked.

"Of course not," Malak answered, wondering for the thousandth time how Amun had gotten so far up in the ghost cell, and how he had managed to remain at large. He was always nervous and shifty-looking. She would have spotted him as a potential threat from a hundred yards away. "You need to relax. You're telegraphing your tension."

Amun gave her a petulant frown. "If you knew what our instructions were, you'd be tense too."

"Take a deep breath," Malak said. "Let's walk."

They started up to the parking lot.

"What are our instructions?" Malak asked.

"I can't tell you yet. All I can say is that it's the most dangerous and complicated mission we've ever undertaken."

"All the more reason to be calm," Malak said with a smile, knowing better than to push him for the information.

Amun returned the smile...finally.

Malak laughed. "That's better. You now look like a Washingtonian enjoying a crisp, sunny day."

Amun had been on edge ever since they entered the country illegally from Mexico, where his friend and mentor, Salim Kazi, had been murdered. Salim had not been a member of the ghost cell. For lack of a better word he was a freelance terrorist associated with several terrorist groups. He was not driven by religious idealism but by his own fame.

When Aaron Lavi videoed the three of them at a Paris café, it was Salim and Amun who tracked him down and killed him. A tactical blunder. Aaron stashed the tape before they reached him. Aaron was an Israeli Mossad agent, and worse, he was the younger brother of another Mossad agent, named Eben Lavi. It was only a matter of time before Eben tracked them down and avenged his brother.

Ziv made Salim's death look like a random killing. Disguised as a Tijuana thug, he confronted them outside of a restaurant the night before they were to cross the border into the United States. A scuffle broke out. When it was over, Salim was dead with a knife in his heart and Ziv was gone.

Malak had no regrets about Salim's assassination. She would have killed him herself if she could have without exposing her cover. And she would have no regrets about killing Amun either, but she needed him. He was the key to finding out who was in charge of the ghost cell. With Salim gone, the impulsive Amun was now dependent on the more seasoned and experienced Anmar. And that was just the way the Leopard wanted it.

"I have a surprise for you," Amun said.

Malak did not like surprises, nor did Anmar, the Leopard. "What is it?"

"If I told you it would not be a surprise," Amun answered. "I think you'll be pleased."

Malak doubted it.

Ziv watched the Leopard and Amun climb into the nondescript Toyota sedan. He waited for them to back out of the boathouse parking lot and pull into traffic before backing his own vehicle out.

He was in no hurry. He had put a tracking device on Amun's Toyota while he was down at the dock. Malak also carried a tracking device cleverly concealed as a clasp on her pack. He only wished she had been able to put a similar device on the woman's car where she had spent the night, or better yet, on her person before she left the house with her two children. But it was too dangerous for her to carry such things around. If a member of the ghost cell found her with a tracking device, they would report it immediately and his dear Malak would be dead within hours or, worse, captured and tortured until she told them what she was doing and what she knew.

Ziv had sent the SOS team on what the Americans might call a wild goose chase, but to his surprise they had found the woman's SUV in the ocean of D.C. traffic. This spoke well of their capabilities. The fact that Eben and Everett had lost the woman and her children at the airport did not surprise him at all. The ghost cell was incredibly well-trained, resourceful, and disciplined. In a way, Ziv was glad Eben and Everett had lost the woman and children. It gave the SOS team an idea of what they were dealing with. If he'd been tasked to track the woman and children, he would have probably lost them too.

Amun pulled the Toyota into a parking garage and Ziv lost the signal.

Here we go, he thought, switching to Malak's signal in case they switched cars or started walking.

Ziv circled the block slowly as if he were looking for a parking space. The third time around he found one, backed in, and waited. Five minutes later Malak's signal came online.

They were on foot.

SATURDAY, SEPTEMBER 6 〉

3:03 p.m. to 5:21 p.m.

Pat Callaghan

Angela, P.K., and I met Mom, Roger, and Bethany in the Solarium. Bethany Culpepper was petite with dark shoulder-length hair, brown eyes, and a warm smile.

"It's good to finally meet you," she said, shaking our hands.

Herbal tea and plates of cookies were set out, either left over from the brunch or baked fresh by Conrad. Bethany talked to us for a few minutes, then took P.K. away so we could have some alone time.

As soon as she and P.K. left, Mom and Roger slumped on the presidential furniture.

"You were smart to skip the brunch," Mom said. "I mean, it was really nice, but we are beyond exhausted. How are you two holding up?"

"Good," Angela and I said in unison.

"P.K. took us on a tour of the house," I said. "He's a nice kid."

"How was your meeting with the president?" Roger asked.

"Brief," Angela said.

"It was nice of him to give you some time," Roger said. "He's a busy man."

At Angela's suggestion we had taken off our Seamasters and put them in our pockets. She said that her dad was sure to recognize the watches as the same model Malak wore.

They talked about the concert the night before, and the upcoming concert in the East Room, and then told us that in order to make the next concert on the tour we'd have to leave right after the East Room concert.

"Boone brought the motor coach over," Roger said. "It's parked inside one of the security gates, and he's getting it ready to go. We'll have to drive all night to get to the next gig."

Mom yawned.

Roger yawned.

Angela yawned.

I stifled a yawn.

Mom laughed. "I guess we could all use a little nap."

We went to our respective rooms. I was in mine only long enough to throw what I'd brought into the White House into a bag and leave. When I got downstairs a Secret Service agent (not Call or Norton) asked me where I was going. I told him I was going to the motor coach. He didn't follow me, but he informed every other agent in the White House that I was coming their way. The agents all nodded as I passed and reported my progress. With the surveillance cameras and agents I figured there were a dozen people watching every step I took. I started to get a little idea of what it must be like for P.K. to live in the "glass house," as J.R. called it. I'd been inside less than twenty-four hours, and I was already starting to feel claustrophobic. And this was from someone who had lived most of his life on a tiny sailboat. How did the First Family do this?

Our motor coach was surrounded by even more security than the Match semi had been. I started toward the door but was blocked by an agent.

"Where do you think you're going?" he asked.

"Home," I said.

The door opened.

"Let him in," the president of the United States said. "It is his home, and this Boone character isn't much of a tour guide."

"Do you want me to ask Mr. Boone to vacate the premises?" the agent said.

J.R. laughed. "Fred, I really hope that no one ever says that to you in your own home. I don't think Mr. Boone voted for me, but he is the driver of the *premises*, and we're having a nice conversation. And I need you to do me a favor. Clear those roadies through the gate. I'll vouch for them."

"With all due respect, sir, you don't know them."

"With all due respect, Fred, I'm the president of the United States. Let them in."

I stepped into the motor coach, and J.R. shut the door.

Boone was sitting at the kitchen table with Croc at his feet. "Thanks for clearing the roadies," Boone said. "And with all due respect, I did vote for you. Twice."

J.R. smiled and joined Boone at the table. "Make yourself at home, Q. After all, it is your home. We're just chewing the fat. Talking about the good old days, which weren't always good, but they were a lot simpler than they are now. How do you like the watch?"

I'd slipped it back on before I came down. "It's great," I said. "Boone told us about the phone number."

"Good. You can call me anytime you want. Well, within reason."

I couldn't even imagine calling the president of the United States to chitchat. "I thought you were going golfing," I said.

"I hate to golf," J.R. said. "But I love walking around the links. It's about the only time I can get outside by myself, more or less, aside from pacing around the Rose Garden. On the way there I decided to take in a few innings of baseball, then I told the Secret Service I wanted to go bowling." He laughed. "That threw them because we have a lane in the basement of the White House, which P.K. and I use once in a while. I told them that I wanted to go to a public alley. We pulled into the lot, and I said that I wanted to go back to the White House. When we got here, which the detail was very relieved about, I saw Ty washing your windshield, and I asked him for a private tour. I think being inside here with the ancient cowboy hippie is making them more nervous than the bowling alley idea. I pull this two or three times a year. You'd think they'd be used to it by now."

"I don't know how you can live in the White House," I said without thinking. "Sorry, I didn't mean–"

"No, you're right," J.R. said. "It's stifling, especially for Will, but we try to keep it as interesting as we can for him. Did he show you the secret passages?"

I didn't say anything.

"I'll take that as a yes," J.R. said. "And the Secret Service radio?"

"You know about that too?"

"The Secret Service is very good at its job. They reported that he lifted one of the old radios immediately. I told them to let him keep it and make sure that he got the encrypted codes once in a while. They also told me he was on the move last night through the passages. Why do you think we gave him that bedroom? That kid is really inquisitive. He found the passages completely on his own, which I knew he would. Norton made sure he didn't roust you from the waiting room until he was sure that Will got the message over the radio."

"Are there other passages?"

J.R. nodded. "But I'm not going to tell you where they are. Ty used one of them this morning to get in and out of the Oval Office, but I had to clear the way so he wasn't caught coming or going. Norton made sure no one would see him."

"Agent Norton has a Seamaster," I said.

J.R. nodded. "Just like yours, Angela's, Ty's, and a couple of other people."

"Pat Callaghan," Boone said.

"Yep, Pat has one."

"I talked to him early this morning."

"You're kidding," J.R. said. "How is he?"

"You don't know?" Boone asked.

"Know what?"

"He's across the street, working the park."

J.R. looked shocked. "How long?"

"Thirteen months."

"Good God! They told me he'd been transferred. I figured he was sent to one of the field offices."

"What happened?" Boone asked.

"I don't know all of the details. We were overseas, and he got into a brouhaha with some big-shot diplomat. Punched him in the nose in front of a few members of the press. Todd sent him packing to keep it out of the newspapers. But you know Pat as well as I do—if he punched someone in the nose, that nose deserved to be punched. I think Charlie Norton had something to do with it too, but Pat took the fall because he doesn't have kids still in college like Charlie. Thirteen months! That has to be a record. Why didn't Pat just call me?"

Boone didn't answer.

"Yeah, I know," J.R. said. "The code. If it wouldn't cause a minor riot, I'd walk across the street right now and drag him back over to the White House."

Boone looked at his Seamaster. "He might not be there."

"As I understand the assignment," J.R. said, "they virtually *live* in the park. There's no other way for them to infiltrate and tease out possible threats."

"He might be getting cleaned up," Boone said.

"For what?"

Boone looked at me.

"Agent Norton asked us for an invitation for Pat Callaghan," I said.

J.R. laughed. "That's beautiful! But if Todd gets wind of it, he'll stop it from happening." He pulled out his cell phone and hit a button. "This is President..." He winked at us. "Right...

My son passed out some invitations to the concert tonight. Oh, good... So everybody checks out? No threats? Good... good... I want everyone on that list admitted. No exceptions unless I *personally* tell you otherwise. Is that clear?... Great... Thank you." He closed the phone.

"The list has already been run through the security and criminal databases, and everyone's been cleared," J.R. said. "I was thinking about skipping the concert tonight, but now I'll definitely be there. In fact, I wouldn't miss it for the world." He looked at his watch. "And speaking of going, I'd better get back to work." He stood. "I've been slacking. I'll be lucky to get done everything I need to get done before the concert."

"One more thing," Boone said. "When I talked to Pat this morning he asked me about the SOS team."

J.R. sat back down, with a concerned expression. "Tell me exactly what he said."

Boone recounted the conversation.

"So he was fishing," J.R. said.

"I think he knew more than he was saying."

"Any idea where he heard the rumors?"

Boone shook his head.

"You could do worse than having Pat join your team," J.R. said. "He's a pro and frustrated about what's going on, and what *should* be going on. You're going to need help with this. Pat can help you." He stood again, started toward the door, then turned. "You know, I have about sixteen months left in my final term. All the talking heads blather on about my so-called legacy. What they don't understand is that the accomplishments I'm most proud of are the ones no one will ever know about. If you recall, Ty, you were involved in several of those when we were at the agency."

Boone nodded.

"I cannot think of a better legacy than to destroy the ghost cell before they destroy us."

The president stepped through the door and closed it behind him.

Boone sat silently for a full minute, staring at the door, then said, "Let's take Croc for a walk."

He didn't have to ask twice.

Angela stepped through the door. "I wondered where you were," she said. "I just ran into the president. What's going on?"

"We're going for a walk," Boone said.

It felt great to get outside, away from all the eyes. I told Angela about the conversation we had with J.R. We exited through the northwest gate, onto Pennsylvania Avenue.

Lafayette Park was across the street. The sidewalk was lined with people who looked more like parade goers than protesters. They had signs, but they weren't holding them up. The signs were propped up next to the lawn chairs or on sleeping bags the people were sitting on. They weren't shouting slogans. They were talking on cell phones to each other or to themselves.

"Which one is Pat Callaghan?" Angela asked.

"Three-quarters of the way down. The guy with the brown sock cap and matching beard."

"It's more black than brown," Angela pointed out.

"Not when it's clean," Boone said.

"Are we going to talk to him?" I asked.

"Not in the park," Boone said.

We crossed the street and walked past the passive protesters. Ten feet before we got to Pat, Boone took a stick of gum out of his pocket and unwrapped it. I'd never seen Boone chew a stick of gum.

Pat stared straight ahead with deep-set blue-gray eyes and ignored us. He had three faded hand-lettered posters behind him.

C.I.A. = CENTRAL IDIOT AGENCY

SECRET SERVICE = NAZI SS (SCHUTZSTAFFEL)

IT TAKES A VILLAGE TO RAISE A CHILD?
HA!
IT TAKES ANARCHY!!!

I wondered if Pat had made the posters himself or inherited them from the previous agent who had the dreaded park duty. As we passed him Croc lay down in front of Callaghan and Boone tossed the gum wrapper at his feet.

"Litterbugs!" Pat shouted.

"Don't look," Boone said, and kept walking.

We took a left at the end of the park and started toward downtown.

"Did you pass him a message in that gum wrapper?"

Angela asked.

"Uh-huh."

"What did it say?" I asked.

"Follow the dog."

Moving quickly now, Boone got his BlackBerry out, checked his messages, then started thumbing in e-mails or text messages. There must have been a lot of them because it took him four blocks to finish. He finally pocketed the BlackBerry, and we followed him across the street to a hotel. He didn't stop at the front desk. Instead, he strolled across the lobby to the elevators and hit the button for the eighth floor.

"Where are we going?" I asked.

"We were too exposed at Blair House," he said. "Too many curious Secret Service agents sniffing around. So we moved our primary operation here."

The elevator door opened.

"Are you sure we weren't followed?"

"Of course we were followed. This is Washington, D.C.," Boone said. "But after what happened in Philly we're running countersurveillance. Felix intercepted our tail—a Secret Service woman probably sent by your friend Mr. Todd. Felix stumbled and spilled a large iced Frappuccino down her blouse, then tried to clean her up. She nearly pulled her service revolver and shot him. By the time she untangled herself from the clumsy Felix, we were out of sight. She turned the corner just after we slipped into the hotel. She's probably down in the lobby right now, flipping her badge open, asking if anyone fitting our description came into the hotel. The clerk is going to say no because Vanessa gave her a wad of money to keep her eyes and mouth closed. The agent is going to be ticked at losing two kids and an old man, and so is Mr. Todd, or whoever sent her after us."

He swiped the card to room 816.

The gang was all there. Well, most of them.

Vanessa was watching a NASCAR race. X-Ray was doing what he was always doing–staring at a computer screen. Everett and Eben Lavi (the rogue Mossad agent who had stuck a knifepoint in my throat twenty-four hours earlier) were cleaning their handguns. Uly, who was only slightly smaller than the gigantic Felix, was playing solitaire. I had yet to hear him utter a word.

"I am sorry about the nick," Eben said, nodding toward the bandage on my neck. "For what it's worth, I would not have killed you."

"That's good to know," I said, although I wondered if he was telling the truth.

"Did the agent come into the hotel?" Boone asked.

"Yep," X-Ray said. He waved us over to his computer and hit a series of keys. We saw us walking across the lobby in fast motion, and then he slowed it down. A woman came in with a brown stain on her white blouse. Just as Boone predicted, she flipped out her badge and showed it to the desk clerk. They spoke for a couple of seconds, and the agent left.

"And our visitor?" Boone asked.

"You mean recruit," X-Ray said.

"We'll see," Boone said.

"He's on his way. Felix is still running countersurveillance, but so far he hasn't spotted anyone following him."

"Is the room set up?"

"Ready to go." X-Ray glanced at his computer. "Speak of the devil."

Pat Callaghan was walking across the lobby with a garment bag slung over his shoulder and Croc at his heels. The desk clerk stared at them but didn't say anything. This was no doubt prearranged because no hotel clerk on earth would let a guy looking like Callaghan and a dog looking like Croc into the hotel without asking what they were doing there.

"Vanessa?" Boone said.

Vanessa clicked off the television. "Wringer time," she said. "If he fails, what do you want me to do?"

"Kick him out," Boone answered. "Tell him to forget about what happened. We'll pack and move to the secondary location before he can tell anyone we're here."

"What are you talking about?" Angela asked.

"Pat Callaghan wants to become a member of SOS," Boone said. "He's passed his background check, which is a little different from the government's background check. All that's left is the final interview. We're going to hook him up to a lie detector. If he gets through it, he's in. If he doesn't, we're out of here. Can't have the Feds raiding our little party."

Vanessa crossed the room and opened the door to an adjoining room. It was completely blacked out except for a bright light shining on a chair across from a desk. On the desk was a complicated-looking machine with leads coming out of it and what looked like a pair of goggles. No sooner had she entered when there was knock.

Boone closed the door to the adjoining room, and we

gathered around a flat-screen monitor connected to a surveillance camera in the black room.

The Black Room

"Come in," Vanessa said from the dark side of the desk.

Pat stepped into the room. "What is this?"

"Sit down."

"What's going on?"

"Do you want to join SOS?"

"Yes."

"Sit down."

Pat sat down.

Vanessa's old but sure hands reached into the circle of light and attached the leads to Pat's wrists and hands.

"Put the goggles on."

"Is this a lie detector test?" Pat asked. "I've never seen a setup like this."

Vanessa did not answer.

Pat took his sock cap off. Underneath was brown hair cut very short. The long dirty brown hair was sewn around the rim of the cap. He peeled off the scraggly beard and tossed it on the table. Underneath was a pretty good-looking guy. He slipped the goggles on.

"Is your name Patrick James Callaghan?"

"Yes."

"You are currently working for the Secret Service."

"Yes."

"You were formerly employed by the Central Intelligence Agency?"

"Yes."

Simple questions like this went on for about twenty minutes. In the upper right-hand corner of the monitor was a graph, which X-Ray was paying close attention to.

"CIA operatives are trained to beat lie detector machines," X-Ray told us. "But no one can beat this one." He glanced at Eben. "Not even our Israeli Mossad friend was able to trick it."

Eben smiled and nodded. He looked less predatory than normal. His jaw was still a little swollen and bruised where Angela had kicked him in the face two days earlier.

"It tracks pulse, eye movement, and pupil dilation," X-Ray said. "You can control your pulse, but you can't control your eyes. They have a mind of their own, and they always tell the truth."

"Speaking of truth," Boone said. "How's he doing?"

"Primed and loaded," X-Ray said.

Boone looked over at Uly. "You ready?"

Uly put down the deck of cards and stood. He was even bigger than I remembered.

"If Pat starts to go south, I want him disarmed, cuffed, and gagged," Boone said.

Uly nodded.

"Remember, though, he's on our side. Don't hurt him."

Uly shrugged as if he couldn't guarantee that and stationed himself outside the connecting door.

"So, you went through this?" Angela asked Eben.

"Right after they took me to the dentist to fix the tooth you cracked."

"Sorry about that."

"I deserved it," Eben said. "And it was a good kick."

Angela had surprised us all with her tae kwon do.

Boone punched a button on his BlackBerry. "Start the real questions," he said into the Bluetooth stuck in his ear.

There was a short pause in the interview.

"Why is Vanessa conducting the interview?" Angela asked.

"It's about to turn into an interrogation," Eben interjected.

"We picked Vanessa," Boone said, "because she's never crossed paths with Pat. If he doesn't pass we want as little exposure as possible. Pat already knows I'm involved in something. We're about to find out how much he knows, and more important—at least to us—where he found out."

Vanessa's questioning resumed, but the yes and no questions were over.

"How did you learn about us?"

"Charlie Norton…well…from him I got at least the notion that you *might* exist. It was purely conjecture on Charlie's part. He mentioned that he suspected President Culpepper was working with a small group of ex-spooks who had gone freelance."

"In what capacity?"

"I don't know. Neither did Charlie. All he knew was that President Culpepper often seemed to know more about the current terrorist situation than the CIA and FBI chiefs briefing him. You can bet both organizations are actively trying to figure out who's feeding him this information."

"Why is Agent Norton interested in this?"

"His job—my job—is to protect the president's life, with our own lives if necessary. And like all presidents before him, he and his staff sometimes make this difficult."

"In what way?"

"By not telling his detail ahead of time what he's going to do. By changing plans at the last minute, like he did today half a dozen times, so they're unable to get the advance and countersniper teams in place. J.R. trusts Charlie and me, but only to a point. He plays his cards very close to his vest. He has a very private, secure cell phone. If it buzzes, he answers it. The only times he hasn't answered it was when he was in the middle of giving a speech or a press conference. As soon as he's finished he asks for a secure room, walks in, shuts the door, and presumably returns the call."

"You and Agent Norton both have that private number."

"Yes we do, but neither of us has ever called it."

"Why?"

"I can't answer for Charlie. As for myself, I've never had a reason to call it."

"Even when you were stationed for radical homeless duty in the park?"

"Absolutely not. At least in my mind. The number's not

used to curry favor with the president of the United States."

"Why did the president give you the watch?"

"Nice try. I'll never tell you why I got the Seamaster."

"What about Agent Norton's watch?"

"I never asked him why he got one, and he's never asked me. That's the way it works. And if he had told me, I wouldn't tell you or anyone else."

"Why were you kicked out of the White House?"

"I punched a diplomat in the face in South Korea."

"That's his first lie," X-Ray said.

Boone passed the information on to Vanessa.

"Why were you kicked out of the White House?" Vanessa asked again.

Pat laughed. "This thing works pretty well."

"Answer the question."

"We were in South Korea at a summit meeting with the president. On the second night there Charlie and I had elevator duty. A guy comes up and says that he has a dispatch to give to J.R. We tell him politely that we'll deliver it. He insists that he wants to give it to the president personally. It's three in the morning. The president is upstairs asleep. Even if he hadn't been, we wouldn't have let him through. He starts yelling at us, then shoves me. Before I can recover he reaches into his pocket and Charlie coldcocks him. At that moment the elevator opens and COS Todd steps out, sees the diplomat splayed on floor, and goes ballistic. Apparently, he knew the guy was coming and failed to mention it to us. The guy comes to and can't remember who slugged him. I told Todd that I did it before Charlie could step up to the plate. He has two kids in college. Next thing I know, I'm across the street. Todd and the Service figured I'd last a month in the park…get a job with another agency. I fooled them."

Boone laughed. "I always did like Pat Callaghan. Is he telling the truth?"

"Yep," X-Ray said. "Looks like that's how it went down."

"Let's go back to last night," Vanessa said. "Were you watching for Boone?"

"Not specifically. Charlie called me on my cell, not the radio. He said that he had cleared the way for an unknown visitor to the Oval Office. He also told me about the kids being taken down there, but I already knew about that because of the radio chatter. He asked me to keep an eye out for a familiar face."

"So, you told him about Boone?"

"I did not. I would never give up a current or former NOC agent, even to someone I trust, like Charlie Norton. I told him that I didn't see anyone."

"Truth?" Boone asked.

X-Ray nodded.

"I recognized Boone in his cowboy boots and Indian hair from a half a block away," Pat continued. "I was shocked to see him, but I played it cool when he walked by. It didn't take a genius to put two and two together. I figured he'd been the secret guest, and that could only mean he was still in the trade."

Boone looked at the other members of the SOS team. "What do you think?"

"We could use the help," Everett said.

The others nodded.

"Finish the interview," Boone said into his Bluetooth.

"Why do you want to join the team?" Vanessa asked.

"I guess for the same reason your team was formed, if I'm right about what your mission is," Pat answered. "I joined the CIA to help protect this country, not to play politics. It would be nice to end my service being part of something that actually is helping the country."

"What can you bring to the team?"

"I can't say for sure until I know what you're doing. But I assume that most of you have been out of the trade for a while. I'm still in it, more or less. My resources are fresh, and a lot of people owe me. I'm not above squeezing them if you need tactical intel. As a former NOC agent, Boone doesn't have these resources because there are only a handful of people in the company that knew he worked there. I operated covert most of my career. I'm still pretty good at tradecraft. And finally, I'd like to actually accomplish something before I hang up my spurs."

"He's in," Boone said, and started for the door.

Before he reached it there was a shout from the interrogation room. Eben and Everett were up in an instant with their guns. Uly threw open the door. Croc ran through. Agent Norton was pointing an automatic at Vanessa, who had a knife in her hand, ready to launch it.

Croc growled and fixed his one blue eye on Agent Norton.

"It's okay, Charlie!" Pat shouted.

"Drop the knife!" Norton shouted.

"Drop the gun!" Vanessa shouted back.

At that moment Felix came up behind Agent Norton from the hallway and stuck the barrel of his automatic against the back of Norton's skull.

"You heard the woman," Felix said.

Agent Norton carefully laid his automatic on the carpet.

Executive Order

"Everyone stand down," Boone said quietly but firmly. He looked at Agent Norton. "You ever heard of knocking?"

"The door was unlocked," Norton said. "When I pushed it open and saw the dark room and Pat looking like he was being sweated, I pulled my gun."

Boone looked at X-Ray and frowned.

"I should have locked it," X-Ray said. "Sorry."

"Who are you?" Agent Norton asked.

Boone's BlackBerry vibrated. He pulled it out. "It's J.R." He pushed the answer button. "You're on speaker."

"Good," J.R. said. "How's everyone doing?"

"Did you send Agent Norton?"

"Yes."

"How'd you know where we were?"

"I'm always watching," J.R. said.

"What do you mean?" Boone was clearly not pleased with the situation, nor was he being very respectful to the man on the other end of the line.

"I just told you," J.R. answered. "Apparently, the only person who's ever figured this out is Malak."

Boone looked at his watch. "You put a tracking device in our watches," he said.

"Bingo," the president said. "And it's not to spy on you. It's to keep track of where my friends are. And the watch doesn't run on a battery. There's a miniature generator inside that's powered by the mainspring. Next time you see Malak, ask her how she knew. You there, Pat?"

"Yes, sir."

"Did they try to recruit you?"

"Past tense," Pat said. "I've been recruited." He looked at Boone and the others. "At least I think I've been recruited."

Boone and the other SOS members nodded.

"Negative," the president said. "You still work for me, but Ty is your boss."

"No way," Boone said. "That's not how I work."

"Hold on, Ty. Hear me out on this."

"I might as well," Boone said, "since you just compromised us by leading Agent Norton here."

"Charlie's working for you too," the president said. "After I left you today, I did some thinking about this. If Pat figured out something was going on, there must be a lot of others digging around. Someone's bound to stumble onto your operation, and it might be the wrong person. Instead of being the hunters you could become the hunted, either by terrorists or the federal bureaucracy. I'm not sure which one is worse. The other problem you have is that you have no legal authority. A couple of Service badges will get you into anyplace you want to go, along with the letter I gave to Charlie before I sent him after you."

Agent Norton reached into his suit jacket pocket and pulled out a sealed envelope.

"The problem is," Boone said, "we don't exactly go by the book. I hate to break it to you, but we break the law on a daily basis. Sometimes several times a day. We play by terrorist rules, which means we have no rules. You're asking two Secret Service agents, sworn to uphold the laws of the United States, to violate their–"

"Let me finish, Ty," the president interrupted. "I've put Pat and Charlie on special assignment directly to me. Their boss screamed bloody murder, but I reminded him that he served at my pleasure, and that if he didn't have the paperwork together by the end of the day, he'd be serving across the street in Lafayette Park, where we currently have a vacancy."

Pat and Charlie both smiled at this.

"You have too much exposure," the president continued. "And so do I. If people want to speculate about where I'm getting my intel, let Pat and Charlie take the heat. Their presence will divert attention from SOS, give you some breathing room, and at the same time give your team some legal authority when you need it."

"Malak was insistent that no federal agency get involved in this," Boone said.

"Malak Tucker's alive?" Agent Norton blurted out. "That's impossible. I was flown in to identify the body at Independence Hall."

"She's alive," Angela said.

"And she's not going to like this," Boone added.

"Charlie and Pat were two of her closest friends when she worked the White House," the president said. "That's why I chose them. They were on the same sculling team."

Pat nodded and smiled at Angela. "We called ourselves the Scull and Crossbones. I can't tell you how happy I am that she's still with us."

"What happened?" Charlie asked. "Why'd she let us think she was dead?"

"She's not quite herself," Boone said. "We'll talk about that later."

It wasn't my place to say anything, but I couldn't help myself. "What about plausible deniability?"

The president laughed. "Is that you, Q?"

"Yes, sir."

"It's a good point. Bringing Pat and Charlie into this leaves me wide open. But as we discussed earlier, I don't care. Even if legal action is brought against me, which wouldn't surprise me, it would take months for them to figure out exactly what I did. I would hope by then the ghost cell would be gone and the country would be safe."

"Your legacy," Boone said.

"Then they're in?" the president asked.

Boone looked at the other members of the SOS team, including Angela and me. We all nodded.

"Charlie's not in yet," Boone said to the president. "He has to pass our little test. If he doesn't pass…"

"Shoot him," the president said.

"Thanks, Mr. President," Charlie said.

Pat put his hand on Charlie's shoulder. "Here's a tip. Don't lie."

"Where are we going?" Malak finally asked.

She and Amun had been moving around downtown for more than an hour and a half. They had been in four taxis, two buses, and several stores. Amun was not usually this cautious about being followed.

They were being followed by Ziv, but with Malak's tracking device he could keep his distance and there was no way Amun would spot him.

"We're about ready for your surprise," Amun said.

The surprise again. This had Malak worried. Amun was not a surprise kind of guy.

Amun looked at his watch for about the fiftieth time since they had left the car in the parking lot. This had her worried too. Amun rarely looked at his watch.

"Are we on a schedule?" she asked.

"Yes," Amun said. "And it's time."

Malak followed him across the street to an old but well-kept apartment building. Amun pulled his baseball cap down, opened the door with a key, and walked through with his face turned away from the security camera inside. Malak followed suit but wondered why Amun was taking this kind of precaution in a private building. Homeland Security did not monitor apartment building cameras. In fact, there was a good chance the old camera in the lobby was just for appearances.

After years of running, stalking, and hiding, Malak's intuition had been honed to razor-sharp claws. The Leopard sensed the stench of trouble in the air. Something bad was going to happen. She was rarely wrong.

Amun took the stairs instead of the elevator. As Malak fell in behind him she reached into her pocket and pressed a button on a special cell phone. If she were ever searched it would look like the battery had been pulled and the SIM card was missing. A dead phone. But it was far from dead. It was her lifeline to Ziv, programmed to dial only one number—his. They used the phone only for dire emergencies. Malak pulled her necklace out from under her blouse. Hanging on the chain was a golden angel and a golden leopard. Inside the leopard was a miniature Bluetooth microphone. Ziv would now be able to hear everything that was being said. She hoped he was nearby.

"So what's this all about, Amun?" Malak asked teasingly. "It's not my birthday."

Amun looked back at her and smiled. "I don't even know when your birthday is. Do you?"

"It was celebrated on February second," she answered. "But of course I doubt that was my real birthday."

"Mine is June thirteenth."

"I suppose birthdays don't matter when you don't exist," Malak said, wondering if June 13 was Amun's real birthday. He had never talked about his childhood or his parents. She didn't know if he had been adopted like her and Anmar, or if he had been raised by his biological parents.

"True." Amun stopped outside a steel fire door.

Malak acted out of breath, which she wasn't—she was in top physical condition.

"Whew," she said. "If I'd known it was nine floors up, I would have suggested we take the elevator." This was for Ziv's benefit, so he would know what floor they were on.

Malak took off her jacket as if she were hot after the climb. The real reason was to have quick access to the backup pistol stuck in the waistband of her jeans, right at the small of her back. As she followed Amun down the hallway she untucked her blouse to make sure it concealed the small automatic.

Amun stopped in front of a door. "Are you ready?"

"How appropriate," Malak said, staring at the number on the door. "Nine-eleven."

"Pure coincidence," he said, and knocked on the door.

A shadow appeared at the peephole, and then the door was swung open by an older man with a smile on his face. He wrapped his arms around Malak and gave her a bear hug. Malak had never seen him before in her life, and she hoped he couldn't feel how fast her heart was beating against his barrel chest. He pulled her into the apartment.

Sitting on the sofa was an older woman. She stared at Malak. She was not smiling like Amun and the old man.

"This is not my daughter," the woman said.

Oh my God, Malak thought. These are Anmar's adopted parents. She tried to remember what the real Anmar had told her about them.

"Of course this is Anmar," the man said. "Look at her! Her hair is different and she's aged, but who hasn't?"

"There were twins," the woman said flatly, her dark eyes neutral but fierce. "Girls," she continued. "Identical. Where is my daughter?"

"What are you talking about?" Malak said. "I don't have a sister. I was an only child. I'm your daughter. You raised me. Your name is Elise." She looked at the man. "Your name is Sean. We lived in a house just off Northeast Halsey in Portland, Oregon. We had a dog named Alfredo."

Malak was stalling. She knew it was only a matter of time before Elise asked her a question about Anmar's childhood that she would not be able to answer.

"I told you this was Anmar!" Sean said.

Elise's expression did not change. "Tell me where you got Alfredo," she demanded.

Here we go, Malak thought. She looked at Amun, who was no longer smiling. "What a lovely surprise," she said sarcastically. "You bring me here to get the third degree from my parents. What were you thinking?"

"Right now I'm thinking about twins," Amun said. He looked at Elise. "Tell me about them."

"As I said, there were two girls. Identical. I saw them at the Beirut hospital where they were born. I arrived first, so I got to choose first. I always wondered what happened to the other girl. Now I know. Who are you working for?"

"I'm working for the same people you work for," Malak answered indignantly. "Why didn't you tell me that I had a twin sister?"

"Because I did not raise you. Now tell me where you got the dog. If you are Anmar you will know."

"Go ahead and tell her," Sean said. "Get this craziness over with."

"You know what," Malak said. "I don't think I will tell her."

Malak had no idea where they got the dog, but she did know that there was no love lost between Anmar and Elise. Anmar despised the woman who had raised her, and it was clear by Elise's cold stare that the feeling was mutual.

Malak looked at Amun. "I will not be subjected to this. It's insulting. I'm leaving." She turned to the front door and disengaged the deadbolt.

"Wait," Amun said.

Malak looked back. "I assume that we've been given a mission. I know you meant well, Amun, but this is a waste of time. Are you coming?"

Amun looked at his watch—again. "We've already completed our first mission. I brought you here to get our second mission. Elise and Sean are my handlers."

Malak had been waiting years for this moment. To take the ghost cell down she had to find out who was running it. She doubted Sean and Elise were in charge, but they were one step closer to the top. She cursed her bad luck having them as the next rung up the ladder.

"What was our first mission?" Malak asked, turning around to better conceal the gun under her blouse.

"The car," Amun answered.

That was why he had been checking his watch so often. The car they had left in the parking structure must have a bomb in it.

Malak wondered why Amun had passed up so many empty spaces, choosing instead to park midway up on the fourth level in the center of the structure.

"When?" she asked.

"Two minutes."

"And that, whatever your name really is," Elise said, "was your last mission." She took a gun from a beneath a pillow on the sofa and pointed it at Malak's chest. "Is she armed?"

"What are you doing?" Amun asked.

"Taking care of a problem that you should have discovered."

"Are you sure, Elise?" Sean asked.

"Positive. Step away from the door," she said, motioning Malak to the left with the barrel.

"This is a joke, right?" Malak said, stepping to the side. "A training exercise."

"You will not be laughing in a few hours," Elise said. "I don't know how you stepped into Anmar's place, but I guarantee that you will tell us."

Elise turned to Amun. "Where does she keep her gun?"

"In her pack," Amun answered.

"Take it."

Amun yanked the pack from Malak's shoulder along with her jacket, then roughly pushed her into a chair—the worst possible position for her to reach for her spare gun.

He dumped the pack out onto the sofa.

A pistol fell out with a suppressor screwed into the end of the barrel. Elise exchanged it for the gun she was holding. "Sean, get my kit. It's in the bedroom."

Sean went into another room.

"Amun," Malak said. "You can't be buying into this?"

Amun ignored her and looked at Elise. "What do you want to do?"

"That is up to your friend. I can shoot her with this gun, or I can shoot her with the hypodermic needle Sean is preparing. It's entirely up to her. We have a van parked in back. Sean?"

Sean did not answer.

An explosion rattled the building.

"Sean?"

Ziv stepped out of the bedroom and shot Elise and Amun.

Car Bomb

The hotel shook. A window cracked, scaring me and Angela half to death. The SOS team acted like it was the twelfth explosion they'd gone through that day, and that included the two new members, Charlie Norton and Pat Callaghan.

"Car bomb," X-Ray said.

"Three blocks away," Boone said. "Give or take."

Vanessa looked at Charlie. "Guess your initiation is going to have to wait."

Boone's BlackBerry buzzed. "It's J.R. again."

He answered. "Right... We're fine..." He looked over X-Ray's shoulder as X-Ray tapped furiously on one of his computers. A picture of billowing dust and smoke filled the screen. "Shopping mall... We'll send people down with Pat..." He looked at Angela and me. "Tell them that they're with Charlie and me, a long way from the explosion. They're safe and we'll have them back at the White House soon." Boone took his phone away from his ear, looked at the screen, then put it back to his ear. "Sorry, but I've got another call. I'll be in touch."

I looked at Angela. "Did Boone just cut off the president of the United States to take another call?"

"Looks that way."

The BlackBerry was back up to Boone's ear. He didn't speak. He listened as everyone watched him in complete silence. I guess they had caught that he had just cut off the president too. Sirens blared outside. Smoke continued to billow from the bombed building on X-Ray's monitor. But we just stared at Boone. He ended the call and looked at the group.

"We've got a little problem."

"I'll say," Vanessa said. "A car bomb in the nation's capital."

Boone nodded. "It's worse. Malak's in trouble."

"What's happened?" Angela shouted.

"That was Ziv on the phone," Boone answered. "It seems that she just met the Leopard's parents, or at least the couple who raised her, and they didn't believe she was their daughter. They're dead. So is Amun Massri. She's been compromised, but Ziv thinks he has a way around it that might even turn the situation to our advantage."

"Wait a second," Charlie said. "Who's Ziv? Amun Massri? By 'the Leopard,' do you mean–"

Boone held his hand up. "Angela and Q can bring you up to speed as you take them back to the White House."

"We're not going to the White House," Angela said. "I want to make sure my mother's okay."

"Your mother is fine," Boone said. "And there is no time

to debate this. Roger and Blaze heard the bomb go off, and they're worried about you. Your job and Q's is to get back to the White House to let them know you're okay. If they start to get suspicious, the game's up. If they find out about Malak, they will pull the plug. Everything she's been through for the past few years will be for nothing. And your parents aren't the only ones asking where you are. Mr. Todd and other staff members want to know too. They're trying to get to your parents, thinking they know what's going on, which they don't. You need to get back there and put a stop to it."

"Your parents don't know about Malak?" Charlie said.

Angela and I shook our heads.

Charlie shook his head too, but for an entirely different reason. "This is unbelievable!"

"Welcome to the dark side," Vanessa said.

"Are you still in?" Boone asked.

"Yeah, I'm in," Charlie said.

"Good. We need you." Boone looked at the others. "X-Ray and Eben are coming with me. Everett and Felix, you're running countersurveillance for us. Vanessa, you stay here and monitor communications. Pat? Get cleaned up. I need you at the bomb site. Use your Secret Service creds. If anyone tries to block your access, tell them you're the president's man on the ground. I'll set this up with J.R. and fill him in on what we're doing. Report directly to him on his private cell. Uly will go with you and fill you in on the situa–"

A second explosion rocked the hotel.

Boone swore.

"Two bombs, same location," Vanessa said. "One for the

public. The second for the emergency workers coming to the
rescue. We have to stop these people."

"Let's get moving," Boone said.

Walk and Talk

The sidewalks and streets were jammed with people, some rushing toward the disaster, some rushing away. We could see and smell the black smoke rising a few blocks from us.

Charlie took us a different way back to the White House than Boone had taken to get to the hotel. It was quite a bit longer. At first I thought it was to avoid the chaos on the streets, but I think his real reason was to give us more time to tell him what was going on. We couldn't talk openly at the White House–too many ears and eyes.

Angela did most of the talking, but I chimed in when I thought she was leaving out something Charlie should know. He let us finish before saying anything.

"You're absolutely certain this woman is your mother?"

"Absolutely," Angela said.

"Sorry that I have to ask these questions," Charlie said. "But I'm a cop. And I'm obviously way behind you on this thing."

"No problem," I said.

"If your parents find out about this, they'll shut down the tour, right?"

"Right," Angela said.

"What's the downside to that?" Charlie said. "I mean, neither of them was exactly starving when they hit the big time. How much money do you need?"

"It's not the money," Angela said. "It's the fact that they gave up just about everything to raise us. Second chances in the music business are rare."

"*First* chances are rare," I added. "And now it's more complicated than that. Boone and Malak think if they drop out now it will create a lot of questions. Reporters will start digging and figure out that Roger was married to a Secret Service agent who was killed in the line of duty. If the ghost cell figures out that Malak took the Leopard's place, they might come after us."

"Witness Security?" Charlie said.

Angela shook her head. "My dad and Blaze are too recognizable. They'd have to undergo plastic surgery and give up music altogether. That's not fair to them. They'll be told everything as soon as the ghost cell is destroyed."

"By the cell's actions today," Charlie said, "that could be a very long time. To pull off something like this in the most secure city in the U.S. means this cell is not only well organized and well funded. It's huge."

"And Malak is the only chance we have of taking it down," I said.

"Do you want to continue?" Ziv asked Malak.

Elise and Amun lay dead where Ziv had shot them. Malak had not been into the bedroom where Sean had gone to retrieve Elise's kit, but she had no doubt that he was as dead as the other two. Ziv never missed and never wasted bullets.

"I might be losing my edge," Malak said, then explained the two lapses she'd had that morning with the coffee and the little girl.

"Losing one's edge is a good reason to give it up," Ziv said. "Boone is on his way over here with Eben. There are two cell members watching this apartment right now. Dirk is watching them. They have no idea what happened here. We could easily take them out, and that would mean five relatively high-up cell members gone from the face of the earth. Not enough to bring the cell down, but it would certainly be a blow to the organization."

They had turned on the television. Every news station was showing the devastation from the bombs. No one knew how many people had died, but the reporters were predicting that the casualties would be in the dozens.

"Or," Ziv continued, "we could take the two watching the building alive and find out what they know, but the chances of them knowing very much is small."

A news anchor came on.

We have just received a communiqué from the Al
Jazeera television network. Three well-known terrorist
groups are claiming to have joined forces to deliver
this coordinated attack against the United States. The
three groups are...

Ziv switched off the television. He'd heard enough. He and
Malak both knew this was not a coordinated attack from three
different terrorist groups. There weren't three terrorist groups on
earth that could get along long enough to pull something like this
off. The attack was the work of the ghost cell, which was happy to
have other terrorists take the credit for the attack and suffer the
consequences. The members of the ghost cell were not martyrs
unless it was absolutely necessary. Their motto was, Live to kill
another day.

Ziv took his cell phone out and called Boone. "Hold off for a
moment. I'll get right back to you."

He ended the call and looked at Malak. "As you already know,
whatever you decide is fine with me. We can end this right now
without any regrets. Turn what we've learned over to Boone, and
then you and I will disappear."

Malak smiled. "Dear Ziv," she said. "Disappear into the sunset
like we're in a western? It's not as simple as that. It never is. Which
is why westerns are so popular and why you like them so much."

"You're right. I'm a romantic at heart," Ziv said, returning her
smile.

"What's your plan?"

"Very dangerous for you as always, but we'll need Boone and his team to help us."

"I will never be safe as long as the ghost cell exists, nor will Angela or Roger or Q or Blaze. I won't give up. I can't. Call Boone back."

Boone, Croc, and X-Ray walked through the front door of the apartment twenty minutes later. Croc sniffed the two corpses, then jumped up on the sofa and lay down.

Ziv was on his cell phone when they entered. "Are they clear?" he asked. He nodded, then ended the call.

"We saw the two watching the building," Boone said. "We're running countersurveillance on them. We'll get some photos and run them through the database."

"We also saw Dirk," X-Ray added. "He sticks out like a sore thumb."

"Where's Eben?" Ziv asked. "He's critical to our plans."

"We thought it best to have him come in a different way," Boone said. "Dirk didn't even pick him up."

Eben stepped out of the bedroom carrying a pistol. "There is an old man in there facedown on the bed with a bullet in the back of his head. Hello, Ziv."

"Hello, Eben. It's good to see you."

"I'm sure it is." Eben looked at Malak, the gun still in his hand.

"I did not kill your brother," Malak said.

"I know." Eben holstered the gun and took a closer look at the bodies lying on the floor. "It would have been nice to keep Amun alive so we could have a talk with him. Did he set the car bomb?"

"Yes," Malak said. "And I was with him. He didn't tell me."

"Perhaps he didn't trust you as much as you thought."

"I think it was this woman who didn't trust me. She was Amun's handler."

"Then we should have kept her alive." Eben looked at Ziv. "Is this your work?"

Ziv shrugged. "We have more important things to discuss."

"Are you sure this place is clean?" X-Ray asked.

"The ghost cell does not use listening devices," Ziv said.

"Let's make sure." X-Ray pulled a piece of electronic equipment out of his backpack. There was a wand attached, which he started running over every inch of the apartment.

Malak looked at Boone. "Is Angela safe?"

"Yes. In fact, she's with an old friend of yours by the name of Charlie Norton." He pulled up the sleeve of his shirt and looked at his watch. "By now they should be inside the White House."

Malak stared at the watch.

"It's an Omega Seamaster," Boone said. "J.R. gave it to me. Charlie has one too. So does Pat Callaghan. So do you, but J.R. says that you've modified yours."

Malak smiled. "In Switzerland, right after the bomb at Independence Hall. I'm just glad J.R. wasn't tracking me while I made my escape. It was sheer luck that I found J.R.'s little surprise inside." She held up her wrist. "The watch was damaged in the explosion at the hall. I took it in to get it fixed. The jeweler found the gadget inside. He didn't have any idea what it was. When he put the watch back together I had him leave it out."

"J.R. gave Angela and Q Seamasters early this morning."

"They're in an exclusive club. How are Charlie and Pat?"

"They're working for us now," Boone said.

A flash of anger crossed Malak's face. "I told you in very clear terms that I did not want—"

"We need help, Malak," Boone said. "It was J.R.'s idea, and I totally agree with the decision. Aside from being your friends, Pat and Charlie are two of the best operatives in the business. They are working for me, not J.R. He needs plausible cover for the information you're feeding him. They're going to keep their credentials. Right now Pat's at the bomb site. There are places he and Charlie can go that we can't. All they have to do is flip their badges out. If they have trouble, J.R. will get them in with executive privilege. You know how it works as well as I do. They want to help you. They want to stop the ghost cell."

Tears welled up in Malak's eyes. "They're risking their lives and careers."

"Apparently, they think you're worth it."

"You're right, Ziv," X-Ray said. "The apartment is as clean as a whistle. I don't understand why they didn't use bugs for a meet like this."

"They like doing things the old-fashioned way," Ziv said. "It's safer. No electronic footprints for anyone to follow. But let's stay focused. We don't have much time.

"After a hit like today's, the ghost cell usually lays low. They go dormant before striking again. Amun said that the bomb was only the first mission. As Malak told you, Amun said that they have people in the White House, and he implied that something bad is going to happen there. The explosions today might have been a prelude of worse things to come.

"I believe that Malak was about to be promoted. Getting past Elise was her last test. If she had succeeded, she would have risen far above Amun, who was an incompetent fool. Elise knew Amun was a fool because Elise has never been anyone's fool."

"You knew her?" Boone asked.

Ziv nodded. "For most of my life, from the old days in Lebanon. She was one of the smartest people I've ever met, if not the smartest. But she was not the head of this cell." He looked at Eben. "I wish I could have kept her alive, but I had no choice. She was about to kill Malak. I didn't know the man in the other room, who went by the name of Sean. And I doubt Elise told him half of what was really going on in the organization."

Boone looked at Malak. "So, you're coming in. This is over for you."

Malak shook her head. "I'm just getting started. I'm in until it's over for them. There's no other way."

"Your handler and your bogus parents are dead," Boone said. "You're done."

"The Leopard is very much alive," Ziv said. "It's time for some terrorist theater. The first act will start outside for the two people watching the apartment." He looked at Eben. "You will have a starring role."

Eben frowned.

"Here's what really happened here," Ziv continued. "A rogue Mossad agent by the name of Eben Lavi, seeking revenge for the death of his younger brother, followed Amun and the Leopard to this apartment complex. After they entered he climbed up the fire escape and shot Sean in the bedroom. Then he came out here and shot Elise and Amun. But the Leopard was too quick for him. His fourth bullet only grazed her left arm. She shot Eben in the right leg, fled the building, jumped into Elise's van, and drove away.

Approximately two minutes after the Leopard makes her escape, you, Eben, will come limping out of the building desperately frustrated at being wounded and losing your quarry."

"What about act two?" Boone asked.

"I'm afraid I don't have that entirely written yet," Ziv said. "The Leopard is going to go to a sympathetic doctor to have her wound treated. These doctors are usually very low in the cell infrastructure. When the Leopard walks in, he or she will treat her with no questions asked. Malak will receive instructions before she leaves the doctor's office, or someone will contact her outside the office. More than likely she will be sent to a safe house to lick her wounds.

"In the meantime the two people outside watching this apartment are going to enter the building as soon as Eben leaves. They will report what they find. Your men will stay and watch. Eventually, a cleanup crew is going to come to the building and remove all evidence of what happened here. I want them photographed and followed. We'll add them to the ghost database. And with luck, following the bodies will lead us to more cell members."

"What if they don't believe the Leopard's story?" Boone asked.

Ziv looked at Malak with sad eyes. "Then they will kill her." He pointed his silenced pistol at her.

Boone grabbed his arm. "What do you think you're doing?"

"I'm going to wound a leopard."

"Let him, Boone," Malak said. "I can't go to the doctor without an actual wound."

"Who are you, Ziv?" Eben asked.

Ziv looked at him for a moment. "I'm the Leopard's real father." He looked back at Malak. "And Malak's."

Then Ziv shot his daughter in the arm.

The King of the Mountain

Mom, Roger, and Bethany were relieved to see me and Angela when we strolled into the Solarium with Charlie. He told them that we were touring the National Museum of Natural History at the time of the explosion and that we were perfectly safe.

"I got them back here as quick as I could," Charlie explained. "It took longer than I expected because of the traffic."

"Dad has called off the concert," Bethany said.

"We're leaving as soon as Boone gets back to drive us to the next venue," Mom added.

"Where *is* Boone anyway?" Roger asked.

"He had an errand to run," Angela answered.

Yeah, I thought. Like saving her mother and the world from terrorists.

Mr. Todd walked in, glowered at Charlie, and said, "The concert's back on. The president just went on national TV and said he wasn't about to have terrorists interrupt the United States government, including the concert planned for the

White House this evening. The concert will be held in honor of those who lost their lives in the attack, and he wants the concert televised. He's soliciting donations that will go directly to the families of those who were lost."

Mom and Roger wrote the first check, a big one, then said that all the proceeds from their concerts for the next two weeks would also go to the fund.

When Buddy T. heard about this, there was a third explosion in Washington, D.C., but Mom told Buddy T. to get over it, they were donating the proceeds, and hung up on him. No fatalities.

The terrorist attack and the fund-raising effort would change the entire tone of the concert. Mom and Roger started discussing how they were going to handle it. I don't think they even noticed when Angela, Charlie, and I left the Solarium.

Charlie said he was going to brief the president and that he would see us later. We found P.K. in his bedroom, watching the disaster on television. He had changed into starched khakis, shirt, polished shoes, and a blazer.

"Guess the concert's still a go," he said. "Bethany made me change into these. Thought I'd be able to take them off. Now I have to leave them on."

"You look sharp," I said.

"Are you going to change clothes?"

"Probably," I said, although no one would notice because Angela and I had several sets of the same clothes, which we wore like uniforms.

Angela put on her sunglasses and lay down on his bed.

"Something the matter?" P.K. asked.

"Nah, she's just tired. All that walking at the museum wore us out."

"Did you see the Hope diamond?"

"Sure," I lied.

"I'm just mad about that rock," P.K. said.

"*Mad* about it?"

"Sorry about that. I went to school in England for a couple of years, and sometimes little Briticisms slip out."

"I kind of like it," I said.

Angela said nothing. I was sure she was thinking about Malak, wondering what was going on. She wore shades most of the time, but this time she might have put them on so we couldn't see her tears.

P.K. pointed to the television. "Terrible thing. They'll blame Dad of course. Goes with the territory."

"How many people were lost?"

"Sixteen so far. Five in the second explosion. It could have been worse."

"They'll catch them," I said.

"I doubt it," P.K. said. "The surveillance cameras weren't working. For the past year graffiti writers have been tagging the parking structure. Before they strike they take the cameras out. It's happened at least a dozen times. The guy who usually fixes the cameras was on vacation, and they couldn't find anyone to take his place. So there's no video of the car coming into the garage, which means this has been planned for a long time. The FBI is looking for the taggers, which at this point is the only lead they have. The press is having a field day with that."

Just before we got to the White House, Boone called Charlie and told him what had happened at the apartment. Charlie wasn't going to share the information with us, but Angela insisted. It took another phone call to Boone for Charlie to give in.

By now J.R. knew exactly who planted the bomb, but he was withholding the information in order to protect Malak. If the FBI and Homeland Security knew this, he would probably be impeached. My admiration for P.K.'s dad went way up. He'd be an international hero if he went on television and reported that the perpetrators had been caught and were currently lying dead in a D.C. apartment. Instead, he was keeping his mouth shut while federal agents were rounding up taggers.

P.K. and I stared at the television as they played the worst footage over and over again and interviewed terrorist experts who had no idea who was really responsible for the bomb.

"I don't get it," I muttered, more to myself than to anyone else, but of course the sharp-eared P.K. picked it up.

"What?"

"I mean, I understand that this is some kind of religious war and that they don't like us and they want to kill us, but what's the point? What's the endgame? What's their ultimate goal?"

"Reinstatement of the caliphate," Angela said without lifting her head off P.K.'s pillow.

"Huh?"

"Angela's right," P.K. said. "At least that's what some people think."

"Great," I said. "What's a caliphate?"

"Several centuries ago the Muslims controlled almost all of the known world," Angela said. "Their leader was called the caliph, supposedly chosen by Allah, or God, to rule his people. The caliph's word was law."

"Except," P.K. said, "after Muhammad ibn Abdullah, the first—and some say the only true—caliph died, there were huge fights over who should rightfully take his place. He founded the religion of Islam, but it seems he passed away without making it clear who his successor was or how he was to be chosen. Several powerful caliphs came and went over the centuries, but there was a lot of infighting among the various tribes and factions. Eventually, this loosened Islam's hold on the world."

"So they're not just interested in destroying the United States?"

"No," Angela said. "The radical fundamentalists, of which there are actually very few compared to all of Islam, believe that the infidels, which includes all of us in this room, need to die."

"It's worldwide," P.K. said. "Dad says that the U.S. is like Wal-Mart. If they can take the big boy down, the others are bound to follow. This didn't start with 9/11. It's been going on for hundreds of years."

"Fine," I said. "So who's the caliph?"

"There are a lot of guys in line for the job," Angela said. "And they are all guys. No girls allowed. But no one can agree on who it might be."

"And now we have people whose daytime jobs are being

terrorists," P.K. said. "It's what they do, it's what they've always done. They don't know how to do anything else. If this war ended tomorrow, what are these people going to do for a living? Get jobs at Wal-Mart?"

"Religion and oil," Angela said.

"Bingo," P.K. said. "Dad says that the worst discovery in history was oil. The only way to get off it is to burn it all up. Only then will we come up with an alternative energy source. If we didn't need oil, we wouldn't be in the Mideast. We could leave the tribes and factions to fight it out among themselves like they've been doing for thousands of years. The only thing we'd have to do is make sure they don't get their hands on a nuclear bomb."

"And protect Israel," Angela said.

"Dad says Israel should be moved to Utah, where we can really protect them," P.K. said. "He's kidding...I think. Don't tell anyone that. It wouldn't go over well."

"Okay," I said. "So this whole thing is like really, really stupid."

P.K. laughed. "Madly stupid. Among the billion or so Muslims there are several thousand committed, well-trained religious zealots who believe with all their hearts they are doing Allah's bidding by trying to kill us." He pointed to the television. "What they don't get is that when they do something like this it really ticks us off. Instead of dividing us it unites us, at least for a while."

I was way out of my depth. "So who do you guys think is going to be the caliph?"

Angela sat up and looked at the television. "The man who

becomes the caliph will be the man who has the most power at the end. It's like the game I used to play in elementary school, king of the mountain."

"I used to play that too," I said. "It got kind of rough sometimes. Did you ever win?"

"I always won," Angela said.

I believed her. She was a lot tougher than she looked.

SATURDAY, SEPTEMBER 6 〉

6:02 p.m. to 6:57 p.m.

Malak climbed into the van in back of the apartment building and drove away with blood dripping onto the steering wheel. Ziv had just grazed her arm, but it felt like a leopard had taken a bite out of it. She couldn't stop to stanch the bleeding because she was allegedly fleeing from the crazed Eben Lavi, who was probably at this very moment limping out of the apartment building with her blood on his jeans. That was the odd little gadget man with thick black glasses they called X-Ray. "Rub your wound on Eben's thigh," he had said. "Otherwise it won't look realistic."

Malak smiled despite her desperate situation. She had wiped her wound on the ex-Mossad agent's leg on the way out the door, with Eben looking as uncomfortable as she felt.

As she fled down the hallway Ziv called out to her in Arabic, "The Leopard found the puppy at a Sonic Drive-In while she and Sean were ordering limeades and burgers."

If Malak survived the day, which seemed unlikely to her at this point, she would have to sit down with Ziv to find out what else he knew about her twin sister. If Malak had known about the puppy, Elise, Sean, and Amun might still be alive.

About a mile from the apartment she pulled into the parking

lot of a drugstore and took her jacket off. In the glove box she found a packet of tissues and bound half the stack to her wound with a strip of cloth torn from one of Elise's blouses. Elise and Sean had their suitcases in the van and were ready to flee in an instant like the experienced terrorists they were.

Malak wiped the blood off her hand with the rest of the tissues. She looked in the rearview mirror and evaluated her appearance. She was pale and wild-eyed, as if she'd just seen two people murdered before being shot herself. That would never do. The drugstore would have a dozen security cameras. She found a leather jacket in Elise's bag and slipped painfully into it, then added a pair of sunglasses and a baseball cap. Malak didn't exactly achieve the soccer mom appearance she was hoping for, but it was the best she could do. The trick now would be to get what she needed for her wound before the blood started dripping out of her sleeve again. She got out of the van.

Moving quickly through the store would draw attention to herself, as would making a beeline for the gauze and disinfectant. Malak grabbed a cart as if she had several items to pick up, pausing once in a while to look at something that she didn't need until she finally arrived at the first-aid aisle. Her bad luck continued. There was a woman there restocking the first-aid shelves.

"Can I help you?"

"Maybe," Malak said. "My son banged up his knees and elbow last night on a skateboard. He's fine—we got him all patched up—but I thought I should replenish our first-aid supplies for the next time he does a header."

"I hate those skateboards," the woman said. "Kids think they're immortal these days."

"They sure do," Malak said, and started pulling what she needed off the shelf.

"How about that car bomb?" the woman said.

"Horrible!" Malak said without hesitation or the slightest hint that she had been in the car that exploded. "I almost didn't go out because of it. But what are you going to do?"

"You're right," the woman said. "Life goes on. But right here in D.C., I guess nobody's really safe. Does your husband work downtown?"

"No, thank God. He works in Alexandria."

Malak grabbed the last thing she needed and put it in her cart. "Thank you for your help."

"Tell your boy to be more careful on the darn skateboard."

"Believe me, I have."

Malak loaded her purchases one-handed onto the checkout belt. As they were being rung up she looked at the prepaid disposable cell phones hanging on a rack near the register.

"Are these any good?" she asked the cashier.

"A lot of people buy them. You get twenty hours of talk time, and you can recharge the minutes with a credit card. At least you always know what your cell phone bill's going to be."

"I have a cell phone," Malak said. "But I'm thinking about getting one for my daughter so I can get a hold of her when I need to."

The cashier smiled. "I'm sure your daughter would prefer an iPhone, but your pocketbook would prefer one of these."

"I guess I'll try one... Well, I guess I'd better take two. My son's two years younger, and I can't very well get her one without getting him one."

"I hear you."

When Malak got to the van there was blood on the shopping cart handle.

Eben limped out of the apartment building with Malak's blood on his jeans. He looked up and down the street wildly, knowing he wouldn't see Malak, but he did spot one of the people watching the building. He was young, maybe eighteen years old, talking on a cell phone as he crossed the street toward the building.

Bad timing, Eben thought.

The boy's eyes went wide when he saw Eben. He snapped the cell phone closed and turned around, but before he reached the sidewalk Eben was on him. Eben had no choice. A crazed, wounded, rogue Mossad agent, bent on revenge for the death of his brother wouldn't hesitate to assault someone who might have seen his prey get away. He had no doubt the kid was a member of the ghost cell and was on his phone, talking to his handler, when he saw Eben come out. His handler had probably told him to go up to the apartment to find out what happened.

Eben dragged the boy into an alley, slammed his head against the brick wall a couple of times, then stuck his silenced pistol against the boy's Adam's apple.

"I will ask one time. If you answer truthfully I will let you live. If I think you are lying, I will kill you right here, right now. Do you understand?"

The boy nodded and looked like he might faint.

"Where did the woman go?"

"I don't know."

Eben cocked his pistol.

"I'm telling the truth! I don't know!"

Eben waited.

"She ran out of the building and went around back. Maybe she had a car. She looked hurt. Her arm."

"Good!" Eben said. He reached down, wiped his hand on his thigh, and showed the boy the red smear. "She shot me in the leg."

He hit the boy in the head with the pistol grip. The boy crumpled to the ground.

I deserve a Tony Award, Eben thought as he limped out of the alley and down the street.

Boone and X-Ray watched the act unfold from the roof of the apartment building. They didn't see what Eben did to the boy in the alley, but they were relieved when they saw the boy stumbling out of the alley, talking on his cell phone.

"Thought he was a goner," X-Ray said.

"Eben is smarter than that," Boone said. "On a different subject, with what Ziv told us about himself, do you think you can find out who he is or who he was?"

X-Ray shrugged. "He didn't give us much, but I'll do some data mining and see what I come up with. And speaking of different subjects, there's something we need that would make our job a lot easier."

"What's that?"

"A military-grade surveillance drone."

"You mean a highly classified multimillion-dollar model airplane?"

"Yep. And I want it off the books. No questions asked if the Department of Defense or Homeland Security picks up its blip."

"You don't want much, do you?"

"Don't worry. I'll put it to good use."

"Who's going to fly it?"

"Me and Vanessa."

"Ever flown one?"

"Nope. But I've been reading up on it."

Boone called J. R. Culpepper on his private line and told him what was going on. When he finished he asked him for a military-grade surveillance drone.

"That's right... No, we don't need an operator, just the drone, and we want it off the grid. If anyone asks who's flying it or what it's doing up in the air, it's none of their business..." Boone ended the call.

"What did he say?"

"He's worried about Malak. He thinks she should have pulled the plug, just like I thought she should. I'm not sure there's going to be an act two."

"What about the drone?"

"There will be a white trailer parked in front of Blair House in an hour. Inside will be a three-point-five-million-dollar drone and all the electronic gear you need to fly and monitor it. Keys to the trailer will be on top of the right tire. Does the intellimobile have a trailer hitch?"

"Yep."

The intellimobile was the SOS mobile communication/surveillance van. It didn't look like much on the outside, but inside was a tangle of electronic gear worth more than the drone.

"You ever pulled a trailer?"

"No, but Vanessa has."

The young guy Eben roughed up and his partner crossed the

street and walked into the apartment building.

"Guess the curtain's up on act two," Boone said. "Come on, Croc. Let's go to the White House and put on a different kind of show."

Malak crossed the Potomac into Virginia over the Chain Bridge and went to the house where she had spent the night with the family. She knew no one would be there. Once the ghosts abandoned a house they rarely returned.

She had left the patio door unlocked. She took a long, hot shower and treated her wound, which was still terribly painful. She changed clothes and put the dirty ones in the wash, with the exception of the bloody blouse with the tear in the arm. That would have to be discarded along with her jacket. She carried only two sets of clothes because that was all that would fit in her pack. Leopards had to stay light on their feet...or paws.

As Malak waited for the laundry she made herself two tuna fish sandwiches and ate both of them. The shower, the food, and the peace of her temporary lair went a long way in soothing her raw nerves.

And I will need all the nerve I can muster for this next part, she thought.

She took out one of the disposable cell phones. She was certain Ziv and Dirk were tracking her and knew where she was, or perhaps Ziv had turned this task over to the SOS team, who seemed to have become indispensable. She smiled when she thought of Pat Callaghan and Charlie Norton. Aside from Angela and Roger, they were the two people she missed the most after she became the Leopard. She checked the time on her Seamaster, and her smile broadened.

J. R. Culpepper. She didn't trust him as much as she did Pat and Charlie, but he was the only politician she'd ever known that hadn't been corrupted by power. Becoming the president didn't seemed to have changed this. He'd gone way out on a limb for her. Malak hoped the limb didn't break and crush them all.

She activated the disposable phone.

Malak couldn't use her laptop, even though it was in her pack. There were strict procedures to follow if you were wounded. The assumption was that you were on the run without access to a computer and e-mail.

It had been a little over an hour since she'd left the apartment. If Ziv's theatrics had worked, the cell's leadership knew that Amun, Elise, and Sean had been executed by Eben Lavi and that the Leopard was wounded. A dozen cryptic calls and e-mails had been sent, but only one or perhaps two people had all of the pieces. These were the people the Leopard was hunting. The only way to find them was to stay on the prowl.

She punched in a number.

"Hey, girl!" a cheerful woman answered. "Can I put you on hold? I'm right in the middle of something. Don't hang up. We need to talk."

A couple of seconds later a text message popped up on the display with an address.

The woman came back on. "Sorry. Are you able to make it to the party?"

"Yes," Malak answered.

"Do you have wheels?"

"Yes."

"Not too far to drive?"

"Fifteen minutes."

"Everything okay?"

"Yes."

"Cool! Expect you in fifteen. Ciao."

Malak shook her head in wonder at the cell's brilliant organization. The hip-sounding woman could have been down the street or in Italy. She had no idea who Malak was or what the problem was. If Malak had answered no to any of the questions the woman would have asked another set of cheerful questions and texted her another phone number to call. If Homeland Security had been monitoring the call, which was highly unlikely, they would have completely ignored it.

Malak turned off the phone, then took it outside to the concrete patio and stomped on it several times. She put the pieces into a heavy-duty garbage bag she'd found in the cabinet under the sink, along with her bullet-grazed blouse and jacket. She took her pack and the bag into the garage and tossed them into the van.

On the way to the address she stopped at a Starbucks, threw the garbage bag into a trash can, then walked in and ordered a latte.

Five minutes later Malak was parked outside a doctor's office in Langley, Virginia. She wondered how the CIA would feel if they knew there was a terrorist physician almost within spitting distance of their headquarters. The cell was not only brilliantly organized, they were bold, or in this case maybe even a little reckless.

Malak sat in the van for several minutes, sipping her latte as she scanned the streets, cars, and buildings. If someone had followed her or was watching the doctor's office, she didn't see them, which meant they were either very good or they weren't there.

She got out of the van and walked into the office. No patients, no receptionist, no nurse—just a saltwater tank filled with brightly colored fish. A young doctor wearing blue scrubs opened a door near the reception area. The name tag pinned to his scrubs said "Dr. Lennox." When he saw her he looked confused, then worried.

"I'm sorry," he said. "If you need an appointment, you can call during—"

"I have an appointment," Malak said. "You were told to expect me."

"But I was told the patient was seriously—"

"Looks can be deceiving. And I'm tougher than I look. Let's get this over with. It's dangerous for me to stay in one place too long. Dangerous for you too."

Dr. Lennox started sweating. It could mean that this was the first time he'd been called upon to stitch up a terrorist. Or it could mean something else. Like the young doctor in the blue scrubs was setting her up with the bad guys or the good guys down the street at the CIA. Neither of which would be good. Malak put her right hand in Elise's jacket pocket and wrapped it around her pistol grip.

"Follow me," Dr. Lennox said.

He led her into a sterile room in back with an examination table.

"Take your jacket off and lie down on the table."

"I'll sit on the table," Malak said.

She pulled out her gun and put it on the paper-covered table, then took off the jacket, wincing in pain as she pulled her left arm out of the sleeve.

Dr. Lennox stared at the gun. "That makes me nervous."

"Good," Malak said. "You make me nervous."

"I'd be a lot more comfortable if—"

"Your comfort isn't my concern. Is this the first time you've done this?"

"Yes," Dr. Lennox admitted.

"It's pretty simple," Malak said. "Patch me up and don't ask any questions. And do it quickly. I'm in a hurry." She pushed herself up onto the table with one arm, the gun next to her right hand.

Dr. Lennox pulled a bright light over and then unwound the bloody bandage around her left triceps. As he examined the gash he dabbed the blood away.

"It's pretty deep," he said. "And there are pieces of cloth embedded in it. I can irrigate and disinfect the wound, and put in some sutures, but I'm going to have to numb the area first."

"Fine."

Dr. Lennox walked over to a counter and filled a large syringe, then came back. "I'm going to administer several small injections around the wound with a local anesthetic called lidocaine."

"Go ahead," Malak said. "But if there's something in that syringe besides lidocaine that starts to makes me dizzy like a sedative, they'll find both of us on the floor and you won't be getting up."

Dr. Lennox's hand trembled. "It's lidocaine."

Malak picked up her gun. "It's a nine millimeter." Her hand was steady as a rock.

Dr. Lennox took a deep breath and began numbing the flesh around the Leopard's wound.

Make It Look Good

We headed down to the East Room, allegedly to see how the preparations were going for the concert, but the real reason was that Angela wanted to find out from Boone how her mother was. This was not going to be easy with P.K. sticking to us like the stars on Old Glory. He was growing more suspicious by the minute. He'd asked us three times if Charlie Norton had really taken us to the National Museum of Natural History. When we swore that he had, P.K. rolled his green eyes like we were the biggest liars on the planet. The kid had good instincts, just like his dad.

When we got to the East Room so many people were there that I thought my new watch was broken and the concert had already started, but of course it hadn't. Most of the people running around worked for the White House. The others worked for our parents' band, Match.

"Looks like the Secret Service let the roadies in," I said, doing a quick head count. "They're all here except for one."

"Yeah," Angela said. "He's probably still in jail."

Buddy T. spotted us and stomped over like he was going to knock us down.

"Where's Boone? What are you doing here?"

Angela and I took a half step backward and said we had no idea where Boone was.

P.K. took a half step forward and said, "I live here. This is my house."

"That right?" Buddy T. said. "For your information, this house belongs to the people of the United States. You're just a renter."

P.K. thought about this for a moment, then gave Buddy T. a small smile and looked at us. "I thought you said your parents' manager was a pain in the butt?"

"We didn't say that," Angela said.

Actually we hadn't even mentioned Buddy T. to P.K., but if we had we would have described him exactly like that.

"He seems okay to me," P.K. said. "In fact, I like him. So would my dad."

I saw something I never thought I'd see. Buddy T. actually blushed. And that's when I knew that Willingham Culpepper could one day become the president of the United States if he wanted to. He had the charm and the guile for the job.

"I think your dad does like me," Buddy T. said, recovering some of his normal bluster. "He caved and let my roadies in."

J.R. did not *cave*–at least not to Buddy T.

"What's the *T* stand for?" P.K. asked.

"That's above your security clearance, kid," Buddy T. said with a smile, then walked off to yell at someone else.

Heather Hughes–tall, blonde, already dressed for the

concert, and the president of our parents' record company—walked over to us. We introduced her to P.K.

"It's a pleasure to meet you, Will," she said, and then looked around the room. "It took me an hour to get through the gate. Soldiers and police everywhere."

"It's just a precaution because of the car bomb," P.K. said.

"Scary," Heather said. "I was in the air when it went off. They closed the airport. I didn't know if they'd reopen it in time for me to get here." She looked around the chaotic room. "Where's Boone?"

"Seems like a president of a record company would be more concerned about her musicians than she would about an old roadie with a gray braid," P.K. said.

Heather smiled. "You have a point, Will. But I've known Boone for more than thirty years. He's one of my dearest friends. The Secret Service said Blaze and Roger were up in the Residence. I checked the motor coach on my way in for Boone, and he wasn't there. One of the agents said that he and Croc had gone downtown. I called his cell. He didn't answer. I want to make sure he's okay."

P.K. was about to say something else when Boone and Croc entered the East Room. They walked over to us.

"How y'all doin'?"

Boone's drawl was back.

"I was worried," Heather said.

"'Bout what? The bomb? I wasn't anywhere near it when it went off. Bet you're hungry after that long flight from the West Coast." He looked at P.K. "You think you can escort this poor starvin' woman to the kitchen and talk them into gettin' her something to eat?"

"I guess so," P.K. said. It was obvious that he wasn't thrilled with the idea, but he was too polite to say no. "What kind of dog is that?"

"A very old dog," Boone said.

"A blue heeler–border collie cross," I said.

"He's missing some teeth," P.K. said.

"Yep, quite a pile of 'em in fact," Boone said.

"Let's get some food," Heather said.

"Try the fried cheese curds," I suggested as they walked out of the East Room.

Boone motioned us over to the only corner that wasn't swarming with people.

"Malak is fine," Boone said quietly. "She's inside a doctor's office right now, getting her arm stitched up. I'm not saying she isn't hurting, but it was only a graze. We had to make it look good."

"Are you sure it's going to work?" Angela asked. Charlie had told us about the charade they had put on at the apartment.

Boone sighed. "If they believe her, she'll be fine. If they don't…"

He didn't have to finish the sentence. The rest of it was written all over Angela's face.

"Why didn't she just give it up?" Angela asked. "Her cover's blown."

"Not quite," Boone said. "But I agree with you. The game she's playing now is more dangerous than the one she was playing this morning. It's a gamble. But everyone who suspected she wasn't the Leopard is dead. The alternative is to be on the run for the rest of her life. And this includes you and Q and your parents. If the ghost cell finds out that your mother is an imposter, it won't take them long to discover that she's Malak Tucker, former Secret Service agent, mother to Angela Tucker, the allegedly deceased wife of Roger Tucker," and–he looked at me–"the stepmother to Quest Munoz. They'll come after all of you."

They'd probably come after Boone and the SOS team as well.

"Who made it look good?" I asked.

"What?" Boone said.

"Who shot Malak in the arm?" I'd been thinking about this ever since Charlie told us about it. It seemed incredible to me that someone would shoot Malak to "make it look good." And how do you just stand there and say, "Okay, shoot me in the arm. I'm ready."

"Ziv," Boone said. "And there's something else you need to know that I didn't tell Charlie. I thought I should tell you personally." He looked at Angela. "Let's go out to the motor coach."

That didn't sound good.

Halfway across the East Room we were intercepted by a shouting Buddy T.

"Where have you been, Boone?"

"Takin' care of business," Boone answered calmly.

"In case you didn't notice, we're putting a benefit concert together for the president of the United States and some of his friends."

Boone smiled. "Looks like you got plenty of help. You're

only missin' one roadie, and he was a complete slacker. No one was sorry to see him hauled off to the can. I signed on as the driver and to ride herd over security."

"The motor coach isn't going anywhere until after the concert. About a third of the people in here are Secret Service Agents with guns. I doubt they need your assistance with security. I feel pretty safe. How about you?"

Boone and Croc locked eyes with Buddy T. "I always feel pretty safe," Boone said.

Croc growled. Buddy T. took a step backward. "Did they give you permission to bring that mutt in here?"

Boone nodded. "Right after I gave J. R. Culpepper a tour of the motor coach and asked him to let the roadies into the White House."

"Oh," Buddy T. said, obviously disappointed, but he didn't let that bother him for more than a second. "You need to give these guys a hand. The concert was on, then it was off, and now it's back on. We're way behind, and it's going to be televised. It'll be embarrassing if we don't pull this off perfectly."

"Can't have that," Boone said. "Tell you what. I'll take these two to the coach to change their clothes. Can't have them dressed like they are now. Might embarrass people. Then I'll come back in and lend a hand."

Grandpa

Boone started brewing a pot of coffee while Angela and I changed into concert-at-the-White-House clothes. Mine looked pretty much like what I had taken off—cargo pants, shirt, running shoes. But they were clean. Angela's looked pretty much the same as well: black jeans, black sweater, gold necklace with an angel on it exactly like the one her mother wore, except Malak had a gold leopard strung on hers next to the angel.

We sat down in the plush leather chairs around the coach's rosewood dining table. Croc crawled under the table and started snorting around for complex protein, but he was destined for disappointment. The coach was a no-meat zone except for the odd burger Angela and I managed to smuggle in when Mom and Roger were conked out in the master bedroom in the back. If a little crumb was to drop from the illicit toxic burger, we would have dived to the floor and fought over it like hungry hyenas.

"Tell us what's going on," Angela said.

"You know your mother was adopted?" Boone said.

"Of course," Angela said. "They disowned her, or she disowned them, when she refused the arranged marriage they set up for her." She bit her lower lip.

I was nervous too, but taking a deck of cards out and messing around with them was more annoying than lower-lip biting. The deck stayed in my pocket.

"I met her real father today," Boone said. "You know him as Ziv."

The monkey that watches the leopard's tail, the Philadelphia cop in Independence Park. Warren Parker, aka Grandpa.

Angela said nothing, but I thought she might chew her lower lip off.

"So," I said. "Malak's dad shot her in the arm."

Boone nodded.

"What kind of father would shoot his daughter?"

"Once Malak decided to stay in play, he really didn't have much of a choice," Boone answered. "He winged her to keep her alive."

Angela was still silent, but I'm sure her mind was traveling at Mach 10, trying to wrap itself around this new revelation... or new relation. We knew for a fact that Grandpa Ziv had murdered at least four people, counting the terrorist in Tijuana, Mexico, who had murdered Eben's brother. I wondered if Eben had thanked Ziv for this. Probably not.

"Would you have *winged* her?" I asked.

Boone hesitated a second, then said, "Yes."

I shook my head in wonder.

"How long has Ziv known?" Angela asked. "How long has

she known?"

"I don't know. We didn't have much time to talk after he"–Boone glanced at me–"*winged* her. But he did tell us how he met Elise."

The details were a little sketchy, but Ziv (no last name, not his real first name) met the now-deceased Elise in Lebanon when he was a university student. They had both been recruited by the same organization.

"What organization?" I asked.

"He didn't say," Boone answered. "But there's no doubt it was a radical Islamic group. Probably a splinter group of Hezbollah–party of God. He was at a training camp in Iran when his wife died during childbirth. Ziv didn't find out about her death until he returned to Lebanon. By then she'd been dead nearly a year. They didn't tell him there had been twins. They told him that a girl had been born, but that she had died too. Ziv believed them and spent the next decade coordinating terrorist activities around the world with great success."

Boone reached down and scratched Croc on the head as the motor coach began to fill with the aroma of strong coffee.

"Let me tell you how I define success," he continued. "And this applies to both the good guys and bad guys. A successful mission is one that causes the most amount of damage to your enemy, and when it's over no one has the slightest suspicion that you had anything to do with it."

"Like when you were a NOC agent for the CIA," Angela said.

"Right."

NOC stands for "nonofficial cover." Before he retired

from the CIA Boone was a NOC agent posing as a roadie. If he'd been caught spying, the CIA would have denied ever knowing him. Whatever jam he was in he would have to get out of on his own.

Boone got up, poured himself a cup of coffee, and sat back down. He took a sip and then continued with the story.

"Ziv heard a rumor about a secret cell that had been formed around the time his wife died. It was made up of elite terrorists, and you got in by invitation only. He began to wonder why he hadn't been invited to join. Then he started thinking about Elise and some of his other friends who had been recruited when they were at the university. At least half of them seemed to have vanished off the face of the earth. Elise had been a good friend to both Ziv and his wife. She would have been at the hospital when his wife went into labor. He wondered why she hadn't contacted him when he returned from Iran.

"He got into the hospital's records and discovered that his wife had died giving birth to twins. Girls. Identical. The record went on to say that the father of the twins was deceased. The girls were adopted the day they were born. The names of the adoptive parents weren't given."

"So he started looking for them," Angela said.

"More than that," Boone said. "He faked his own death, very much like your mother did when she took Anmar's place. Like her, he also defected to the other side, becoming a NOC agent for the Israeli Mossad. At least that's what we think. This was the only way he could find out what the Mossad knew about this secret cell. This was also how he managed to infiltrate Eben's mission to track down the Leopard and kill her."

"Did he find Anmar before she died at Independence Hall?" Angela asked.

"He didn't say, but I suspect he did. He knew things about Anmar's past that Malak didn't know."

"This is confusing," I said, and I wasn't embarrassed to admit it.

Boone smiled. "It's supposed to be confusing, Q. Life is not two sheets of paper, one black, one white. Life is a ream of paper, each page a different shade of gray."

That was about as poetic as Boone had ever been. And I was still confused.

He looked at Angela. "One thing I know for sure, Ziv will do everything he can to protect you and your mother."

I wanted to shout, *What about me?* Instead I said, "Malak's not making it easy for him."

"True," Boone said. "But she's getting him closer to his goal, which is finding the people who kidnapped his daughters."

"So he's definitely on our side," Angela said.

Boone shook his head. "Your grandfather is on whichever side suits his purpose."

Dr. Lennox finished suturing the wound and then wrapped it.

"Do you want a sling?"

Malak nodded. Slings, bandages, and casts attracted attention. But a sling was also a good place to stash a small pistol.

Dr. Lennox handed her a vial of pills.

"Antibiotics," he said. "Not poison capsules. Take two a day. It's a nasty wound. If it gets infected you could lose your arm."

Malak stuffed the bottle into her pack and hopped off the table with the gun in her hand.

"Don't worry, Doc. I'm not going to shoot you. The next time you have to patch up someone like me, it will be easier. You can get used to anything. Even patients brandishing pistols."

"I suppose," Dr. Lennox said, but he didn't look like he believed her.

Before leaving the examination room Malak locked eyes with the young doctor until he looked away. The stare was meant to intimidate, but it was also a small indulgence that helped to remind her whose side she was on.

When she met a new cell member, no matter how insignificant their role, Malak imagined herself throwing them to the ground, wrenching their arms behind their back, and cuffing them—not too gently—as she placed them under arrest.

Malak knew this was pure fantasy. She and Ziv had identified dozens of cell members. When the other members were finally apprehended it would be by a coordinated operation involving several law enforcement and intelligence agencies. They would hit the ghosts at the same moment, and it was unlikely that she would be in on any of the arrests. She was no longer a Secret Service agent, and she was no longer herself. The Leopard would be in an interrogation room, a cage, or lying in a stainless steel drawer in a morgue.

Malak left the examination room and clinic without looking back.

Elise's van was gone. In its place was an SUV. Silver with tinted windows.

The back door swung open. Without hesitation Malak crossed the street, climbed into the backseat, and closed the door.

Two men in front, who did not turn to look at her. One behind her, who slipped a black hood over her head. "Gun," he said.

"It's in the pack," she said.

He took the pack and rummaged through it. The SUV pulled away from the curb.

This was not the first time Malak had been hooded. She didn't like it, but she understood the precaution. They didn't trust her yet. They were taking her to a secret location. If they were going to torture and kill her, they probably wouldn't have bothered with the hood. Dead people don't talk. They had allowed her to get into the SUV on her own. The man in back had not patted her down for a backup weapon. All good signs.

Malak had noted the time when she got into the SUV, but that would do her little good in figuring out where they had taken her. Terrorists rarely took a direct route anywhere. They might drive for an hour to get to a location three blocks from where they started.

She said nothing. People who were nervous talked. People who didn't talk made other people nervous.

SATURDAY, SEPTEMBER 6 〉

6:57 p.m. to 7:45 p.m.

Off the Grid

As we stepped out of the coach, I snapped a picture on the q.t. with my iPhone of the sun setting and the Secret Service agents. When I held the phone up, no one knew if I was texting, e-mailing, or playing a game. It didn't occur to them that I might be taking their photo.

People were already starting to line up outside the gate, even though the concert didn't start until eight.

Pat Callaghan pushed his way to the front of the line. After flashing his badge and getting a little guff from the uniforms, he was let through. He looked a little more presentable than he had as a protester but not by much. His short brown hair was covered in dust and debris, and his suit was smeared with dirt from crawling around the parking structure where the bomb went off.

He walked over to us. "How you doing, kids? Mind if I have a word with Boone alone?"

Angela and I looked at Boone.

"They're on the team," Boone said. "No secrets between

us."

Pat shrugged and proceeded to tell us what he and Uly had discovered at the parking structure, which didn't add much to what we already knew.

"It could have been far worse," Pat said. "They could have parked at a different place at a busier time and killed a lot more people. The hard part was getting that much explosive material into D.C. It's as if they pulled their punch."

Boone nodded. "It's a message. No one's safe. Not even in the nation's capital. For the next few days people will hesitate before going to the mall. I wouldn't be surprised if there were more car bombs in different cities. It's not the number of people the bombs kill. It's the fear and terror. They're letting us know that ghosts actually exist."

"Speaking of ghosts," Pat said. "I ran into X-Ray across the street, hooking a trailer up to a van. He told me to tell you that they lost track of Malak."

Boone frowned. "How'd that happen?"

"Three car switches. Lost her on the third. All her cell phones were tossed out the window, and they found her laptop in a Dumpster. Hard drive removed. Her guy Ziv, I guess his name is, told X-Ray that she and he had an emergency backup communication, but that's out too. She's completely off the grid."

Boone swore.

I took Angela's hand.

Malak knew she was off the grid.

The crew driving her made every operative and terrorist she'd ever worked with look like amateurs. The man in back did not go through her backpack; he systematically tore apart the pack and everything inside it. She heard him crush the cell phones and felt the rush of air as he opened the window and threw them out, along with other items from her pack. About a block later he threw the pack out, along with the tracking device hidden inside. She was lucky he hadn't found the device as he tore the pack apart.

Before Malak was transferred to the second vehicle—which seemed to be inside an empty warehouse—they found the cell phone in her back pocket and the gun stashed in her sling. They said nothing as they took them away, nor did she. It was then that Malak knew that she was completely on her own. A few minutes after the third vehicle exchange, she heard the hum of an electric garage door opening and then closing behind them.

She was led through a kitchen with the smells of a dinner being cooked and down a steep staircase. A carpet at the bottom. Cigarette smoke. The crinkle of heavy-duty plastic underfoot as she was made to sit in a hard wooden chair.

The plastic had her worried. Plastic was used to protect carpet from stains such as blood.

The black hood was pulled off her head, replaced by the cold steel of a pistol touching the back of her head. She squinted at the bright white light pointed at her face from a foot away. Beyond the light was blackness. The only sound was the breathing of the person standing behind her.

A full minute passed, then a man beyond the light said, "Tell me what happened." He had a slight Middle Eastern accent.

Malak told him everything from the moment she left the safe house until she stepped out of the doctor's office.

"How did Eben Lavi find you?"

"I have no idea. He might have been following Amun."

"Did you know that Eben Lavi sent his two Mossad agents back to Israel with word that you were dead and buried in a shallow grave at a farm outside Philadelphia?"

"No."

The fact that the man knew this meant that the ghost cell had done the impossible: they had infiltrated the best intelligence agency in the world.

The man continued. "Eben also sent with them his official resignation from the Mossad."

"Apparently, he lied," Malak said. "Or else he's gone rogue on them."

"Tell me about Amun," the man said.

"Amun was a liability," Malak said. "He was a fool."

"Amun was my son," the man said.

Malak hid her surprise. The revelation explained how Amun had risen to his position within the cell.

"I'm sorry for your loss," Malak said. "But Amun was still a fool. He was reckless. He should never have been put in the position he was in. He compromised our cell on a daily basis."

This was followed by a longer silence. All the man beyond the light had to do was nod and Malak would be dead. They would wrap her corpse in the plastic under her feet and haul it away.

Showdown

Angela was in bad shape as we walked back into the East Room. Pale, shaky, worried-looking—which was natural under the circumstances. But we couldn't afford to look this way. Pale, shaky, and worried would lead to questions we could not answer without blowing Malak's cover and ruining our parents' music careers.

I was relieved to see that Mom and Roger weren't down from the Residence quarters. One look at Angela and they would know that something was terribly wrong. The room had emptied out except for a few roadies, camera operators, and Secret Service agents.

I held Angela back as Boone and Pat walked ahead.

"Get a hold of yourself," I whispered. "Malak is tough. She knows what she's doing."

"So does the ghost cell," Angela said. "When things went bad in the apartment she should have thrown in the towel. Even Boone's scared. I could see it in his eyes."

"He's not scared," I said. "He's concerned. I know the

difference. The only time I've seen him scared was in Philly when you ran away."

"He was scared?"

"Petrified, and mad. You shouldn't have–"

"Let's stay on subject," Angela interrupted. "My mom's totally on her own now. No one knows where she is."

"They'll find her. Or she'll find a way to get in touch with Ziv or SOS. This can't be the first time she's walked a tightrope without a net."

"Maybe so, but she's teetering, and if she falls…"

"What are you doing in here, Agent Callaghan!" Chief of Staff Todd shouted. He started across the room, flanked by two skinny aides in suits. His chest and jaw were jutting out like he was going to tackle Callaghan. His surly bluster reminded me of Buddy T. I wondered if they were related.

Patrick James Callaghan gave Todd a wide grin, no doubt thinking about the dozen ways he could snap Todd's neck with his bare hands.

The good thing about the confrontation was that it was taking Angela's mind off her mother. In fact, everyone in the room had stopped what they were doing and were staring at the impending collision.

P.K. joined us with Heather, who was dabbing cheese curd residue from around her lips. Heather was an addicted runner. I wondered how many miles she was going to have to run to burn off the nine thousand calories from Chef Conrad's specialty.

"Where have you been?" P.K. asked.

"Out in the coach, changing," I said.

"Your clothes look the same."

"They are the same, but they're clean."

Todd had closed the gap to about fifty feet and was still charging forward like a bull.

"You're going to want to watch this," I said to P.K. "Your dad wanted to see it, but he's not here. You'll have to describe it to him."

Pat squared his body toward the charging Todd and shifted his weight to the balls of his feet.

Todd stopped two feet away. His red face looked hot enough to explode.

"You didn't answer my question, Agent Callaghan!"

"I guess you didn't get the memo," Pat said cheerfully. "Maybe your security clearance isn't high enough. I've been put on special assignment to the president of the United States. I'd tell you what it entails, but then I'd have to kill you. Which of course would be a shame because you're so likable."

"We'll see about that!" Todd drew his cell phone from his pocket, flipped it open like a switchblade, stabbed a button with his thumb, and stuck it to his ear. "I need to speak to the president... I know he's in a meeting in the Situation Room! Who do you think you're talking to? This is important." He waited a second with a confident, nasty grin on his face. "What? Did you tell him it was important?" His grin faded. He snapped the cell phone closed and pocketed it.

"Busy, huh?" Pat said. "Let me give it a shot." He took out his cell phone, pressed a button, and waited about two seconds. "Sorry to bother you, sir." He winked at Todd. "I'm in the East Room, and apparently Mr. Todd is confused. I think he wants to toss me out of the White House." He looked at Todd. "Yeah, I'd say so... No, he hasn't tried that yet, but I think he'd like to..." Pat laughed. "No, sir. I'd never do that to a member of your staff unless I felt that your life or mine was threatened... Right, I will."

He held out his phone to Todd. "It's the president. He'd like to have a word with you."

Todd grabbed the phone. "Right, but–Right, but–How do you expect me to–Right, but–Hello? Hello?"

"Dropped signal, huh?" Pat said, grinning. "Guess I need to get a different service provider. Or maybe Peregrine hung up on you." He held out his hand for the phone. Todd slapped it in his palm and walked away.

"What was that all about?" Heather asked.

Pat gave her a broad smile. "That was the most beautiful moment of my Secret Service career, Miss..."

"Hughes...Heather Hughes." Heather's face flushed.

Pat turned a little red too. For a second I thought he was going to kiss her. It didn't look like Heather would mind.

"My name's Patrick Callaghan, but you can call me Pat." He looked at his watch. "Would you like a private tour of the White House? I think there's time before the concert."

"That would be wonderful," Heather said.

They walked away, smiling at each other as if we didn't exist.

"My son was perhaps a little impulsive," the man beyond the light said. "But he was a great warrior for Islam."

"Then your son is in paradise now," Malak said.

Was the man Amun's real father? Amun had never mentioned him. She'd always assumed that he had been raised by an adoptive family as she had been. Perhaps she had misjudged Amun. He had never said a word about the man behind the light.

It was Amun who had placed the bomb at Independence Hall that killed her sister. It exploded as Anmar was trying to disarm it. Amun had bragged to Malak about the bomb. He said that it had killed dozens of people, but the only person who died that day was her twin sister. She remembered the conversation well—Amun grinning as he told her about joining the school group touring the building and placing the backpack with the bomb inside. As she had listened, it was all she could do not to kill him on the spot.

"Of course you know that Elise was my younger sister," the man said.

Here we go, Malak thought. The question game Elise started is about to continue.

Malak and Anmar had spent hours talking about Elise and

Sean. Anmar would have told her if Elise had an older brother. If the man were Elise's brother, providing she could get the information to Ziv or SOS, they would be able to find out who this man was.

"Elise never spoke about her family," Malak said. "I didn't know she had a brother." She thought about saying that she was sorry about Elise's death, but the truth was that she wasn't sorry, and the Leopard wouldn't be either.

This was followed by another long silence.

"How long were you at the apartment before Eben came in?"

"No more than ten minutes," Malak answered. "Which you no doubt already know. I assume you had spotters outside the apartment. How did Eben Lavi get past them?"

Interrogating the interrogator.

It didn't work.

The man answered her question with another question.

"Who did Eben kill first?"

"Sean. He was in the bedroom. Eben came out of the bedroom and shot Elise and then Amun. I think I hit him in the leg. As he went down he got me in the arm."

"Why didn't you finish him off?"

"Eben was behind a chair, well covered. I couldn't afford an open gun battle. Did the spotters take him out?"

"No."

"Why?"

"He got the drop on one of them."

"Where is he?"

"I imagine he's getting the bullet you put in his thigh removed. We will find him."

No you won't, Malak thought. But she was relieved. Ziv's smoke and mirrors had worked. She might just live another day.

"What did you and Elise talk about before Eben arrived?"

Malak knew this was coming. If Elise was the man's sister she would have shared her suspicions with him.

"She told me that I had an identical twin sister and accused me of being her. Apparently, your younger sister was crazy."

"You do have a twin sister," the man said.

"Where is she?"

"We don't know."

"Where are the adoptive parents?"

"Lebanon. But they severed all ties with her years ago. They have no idea where she is either. We're looking for her."

Malak gave a harsh laugh. "Well, you're not looking at her now."

Romance

Boone wandered away to check equipment and talk to the roadies leaving P.K., me, and Angela alone.

"How did Heather like the curds?" I asked.

"She liked them," P.K. said. "But not as much as she liked Agent Callaghan."

Again, P.K. didn't miss anything. He looked at Angela. "What's going on?"

"Huh?" Angela said.

"You look like your dog just got hit by a car."

That was a pretty accurate description.

"I'm just tired," Angela said. "And I don't have a dog."

P.K. shook his head. "No offense, but you're lying."

He was right about that too.

"I can't tell you what's going on," Angela said.

I couldn't believe she said that.

"Why?" P.K. asked.

"Because it's personal," Angela said, and walked away.

"Whoa," P.K. said.

We watched her leave the East Room.

"Girls," I said.

"What do you mean?"

"Her boyfriend just texted her and said that he was going out with another girl."

"Oh," P.K. said, but he looked confused.

I'd just stumbled onto the one thing he wasn't a complete expert in.

"She liked him," I said.

"She can get another boyfriend," P.K. said.

"Yep, but it's a little hard on tour like this. We're not anywhere long enough to really get to know people. We're in a different city every day."

"Bethany had a boyfriend," P.K. said. "But when she took Mom's place here, he dropped her. She was messed up for days."

"There you go," I said. "Angela will be all right in a couple of days."

And by then we would be long gone.

"Elise was convinced that you were not Anmar," the man said.

"When I was eighteen Elise was convinced that I wouldn't make it through my training," Malak said. "She was convinced that the only thing I would contribute to the jihad were warrior babies. Elise was jealous of my capabilities. She was jealous of my success."

"Tell me about Alfredo," the man said.

"My dog?"

"Yes."

"Elise asked me about him too. Eben Lavi shot her before I was able to answer her. Sean and I found Alfredo."

"Where?"

"The Sonic Drive-In down the street from our house. He and I went there at least once a week to get limeades and burgers."

"Why did you name him Alfredo?"

"Because he had white fur. Sean and I both loved fettuccine Alfredo. Elise hated it. And she hated the dog almost as much as she hated me."

"Elise could be difficult," the man said. "She was not happy with the role she was given. She felt she could have contributed more to the organization in another position."

Malak did not respond. This explained a great deal about Anmar's adopted mother. Malak's twin sister had told her that Elise was an intelligent but frustrated woman. She took out this frustration on Anmar and Sean.

"How is your arm?" the man asked.

"A flesh wound," Malak answered.

"The doctor said it was deep."

Malak started to remove her sling. She felt the pressure of the pistol's barrel increase but continued, dropping the sling on the plastic beneath her feet. She flexed her arm twice, keeping her face neutral despite the searing pain.

"Excellent. After the loss of Amun and Elise I thought we would have to scratch this mission. The car bomb this afternoon was just a prelude. Before I tell you about the primary mission I must warn you that if you fail us tonight, this will be the Leopard's last hunt. Because of Elise I still have my suspicions about you. But if you succeed, you will be brought into our inner circle..."

As the man outlined the assignment, Malak found it more difficult to keep her expression neutral than she had when she flexed her wounded arm. Amun had not been exaggerating when he'd told her that today would be a day no one in the United States would ever forget. Unless Malak could keep everyone from knowing about it...

SATURDAY, SEPTEMBER 6 >

7:45 p.m. to 9:16 p.m.

The Itch

I took my iPhone out and texted Angela.

You OK?

Fine. I'm hiding out. Trying to pull myself together.

Good.

Is P.K. w/you?

Yeah. I told him that your boyfriend jilted you.

I don't have a boyfriend.

That's right. He just dumped you, which is why you're upset.

Ahh...I get it now. Tragic. Next time you see me I'll be over that creep.

I never liked him anyway. ☺ They're letting people into the concert. It's jammed.

I'll be there soon.

I put the phone in my pocket and wondered what the SOS team thought of that exchange if they were monitoring it, which they probably were.

"Is Angela coming back for the concert?" P.K. asked.

"Of course. She just needs some time alone."

P.K. and I had moved to one end of the room to watch people jockeying for positions close to the stage. The first people into the East Room were mostly the White House staff we had invited, along with their wives, husbands, girlfriends, or boyfriends. I guess they knew to get there early before the VIPs took all the good spots.

There were a lot more people than I anticipated, and by the serious expressions on the Secret Service agents' faces and the amount of shirtsleeve chatter, there were a lot more people than they wanted jammed into one room.

Wayne Arbuckle spotted us and came trotting over.

"Hello, Quest. Hello, Willingham. How are you?"

"Fine," I said.

Arbuckle looked at P.K.'s blazer, creased khakis, and starched shirt. "You look handsome, Willingham."

"It's Will," P.K. said.

Arbuckle ignored him and frowned at how I was dressed. "Where's Angie?"

"You mean Angela?"

The frown deepened.

There was something different about Wayne, something in his eyes. They were darting around like a couple of flies that couldn't decide where to land.

"Angela is freshening up," P.K. said.

Freaking out is more like it, I thought.

"Where's Bethany?" P.K. asked.

Arbuckle looked at his watch. "She'll be down soon. Oh… I just ran into Chef Conrad. He said he needed you in the kitchen."

"Cheesy?" P.K. said. "I was just in the kitchen. What does he want?"

Arbuckle shrugged. "I don't know. But he said it was important."

"I guess I'd better go." P.K. looked at me. "You want to come?"

I did want to go with him and pop a couple of deep-fried cheese curds into my mouth, but I felt compelled to stay right where I was because I felt *the itch*.

"I think I'll wait here for Angela."

P.K. and Arbuckle walked off in different directions.

The itch.

It wasn't exactly an itch, but that's what I called it. I'd never told anyone about this strange sensation because it had happened only a few times. The last time I'd felt it was on the sailboat a couple of months earlier. I woke up in the middle of the night and had an uncontrollable urge to lock all of the hatches. Aboard or away, we never locked the hatches. As soon as I clicked the last latch closed, my real dad, Peter "Speed" Paulsen, let out a drunken shout from the dock. He tried the hatches, and when they didn't open he tried to beat his way in with an aluminum baseball bat, which he must have brought with him because there wasn't one on deck.

After he was arrested and hauled away, Mom said it was lucky I heard him coming and locked up before he got inside. The truth was, I hadn't heard him coming. When I got out of bed it was dead calm outside, dead silent—until my maniac biological dad showed up.

Was Dad going to crash the White House concert? Would his fame as the best lead guitarist in the world get him through the gate despite his criminal record? Or was the itch about something else? The itch wasn't always followed by something bad, but I had a bad feeling about this one. It was strong enough to make me pass up deep-fried cheese curds.

I started after Arbuckle, who was expertly weaving his way through the crowd to the doorway where everyone was coming in. If anyone knew if my dad had gotten himself an invitation, Arbuckle would. When I was about fifteen feet away he stopped in front of a woman. He gave her a hug and a ten-foot kiss. I was five feet away when they parted.

"Mr. Arbuckle?"

He turned around and glared at me. And for the second time that day his mask slipped, and I got a clear look at the real Wayne Arbuckle. It was a dangerous face. The face of a fanatic. He pushed the mask up quickly, but it was too late. I saw him.

"Q!" he said with a smile. "I'd like you to meet my wife, Lillian. Lillian, this is Quest, Blaze Munoz's son."

I looked at Arbuckle's wife. She was smiling too. She had black hair down to her shoulders. Brown eyes. She was wearing a lot of makeup. The itch had nothing to do with my dad. The woman was not Wayne Arbuckle's wife. The woman looking at me with the bright smile was the Leopard.

"Oh, look, Wayne," she said, pointing. "There's Bethany Culpepper."

Arbuckle looked conflicted. "I guess I'd better go," he said. "I'll bring Bethany over to introduce you."

"Go," Lillian said. "Do your job, honey. I can take care of myself."

Wayne nodded and hurried away.

"Smile, Q," Malak said. "You look like you've seen a ghost. Act like we're having a delightful conversation. Lead me over to the refreshment table, where we can talk privately."

As I led her over to the table with a frozen smile on my face, I desperately looked around for Boone, Pat Callaghan, Charlie Norton–anyone I could pass the Leopard off to. But I didn't see any of them.

Lillian

Malak picked up a small plate, loaded it with appetizers, then stepped to the right of the table, where no one was standing.

"Where's Boone?" she asked.

"I don't know, but I can find him."

Malak shook her head. "It's too late. We're out of time."

"What do you mean?"

She didn't answer.

"Where's Angela?"

"She's here."

"In the East Room?"

"No. She's somewhere in the house, trying to pull herself together. We just heard Ziv and SOS lost you. We thought you might be dead."

"If I don't pull this off, I might be dead. My loyalty is being tested. It's imperative that I don't see Angela. If you recognized me, she'll recognize me. You need to make sure she doesn't get close to me."

"I don't have any control over Angela!"

"Keep your voice down and keep smiling."

I smiled but it wasn't easy.

"If Angela sees me, her reaction might blow my cover. If I see her, *my* reaction might blow my cover. If that happens, I'm dead–and so are Bethany and Will Culpepper."

"What?"

"They are going to be kidnapped. Failing that, they'll both be killed."

"I thought the White House is the most secure building in the world," I said.

"Getting in," Malak said. "Not getting out. My job and Arbuckle's is to get Bethany Culpepper out. A man named Conrad is going to snatch Will Culpepper."

"Chef Conrad is a mole?"

"He's a chef?"

"Yeah, and P.K–Will–is in the kitchen with him right now."

Malak swore. "You need to get him back in here, and don't leave his side until this is all over."

"What if he's already taken him?"

"He hasn't. It's not time yet. But he's probably staging the kidnap right now. The ghost cell is going to get only one Culpepper tonight, and it's not Will. I'm not going to allow them to take a child."

"P.K.'s young," I said, "but he's not a child. How about if we put an end to all of this right now by telling the Secret Service about the plot and arresting Wayne Arbuckle and Conrad Fournier?"

"Because it wouldn't put an end to anything," Malak said

sharply. "Arbuckle and Conrad don't know anything. They are following orders from someone they've never met. They don't even know how they got their positions here, which means they aren't the only ghosts in the house. There's a mole, or moles, much further up the food chain, and they are probably watching you and me right now."

I thought about what P.K. had said about Conrad. His dad had insisted that he be hired over the objections of *almost everyone* in the house. J.R. was not a mole. Those who had supported Conrad's being hired would narrow the top mole list down significantly.

"I have to make this short," Malak continued. "You and Angela have to make sure that P.K. is safe. Even if that means physically restraining and hiding him if he resists."

She smiled and handed me her plate. There was a folded piece of paper under it. It seemed Angela's mother was pretty good at sleight of hand because I hadn't seen her put it there.

"After this goes down," she said quietly, "you need to get this note to Boone as soon as you can. He's to pass it on to the president ASAP. Nothing–and I mean nothing–is to be done until J.R. reads this note. You'll find Arbuckle either dead or unconscious in the Library, on the ground floor. He needs to be taken out of the White House without Secret Service knowledge because we don't know who we can trust. Charlie Norton and Pat Callaghan will know how to pull this off."

"You're getting Bethany out of the White House through the Library," I said.

Malak smiled but this one looked genuine. "Smart boy. The ghost cell has good inside information, but their plan is flawed. I've made some adjustments." She looked across the East Room. "This used to be my house."

The Leopard padded away and disappeared into the crowd.

The Note

Chef Conrad a mole? Was Malak lying?

I headed for the door, wondering if I should try to find Boone first to pass the note to him before grabbing P.K. The note...

I stopped and looked around. No one was paying attention to me. They were all looking at Arbuckle, Bethany, and the stars—aka Mom and Roger—who were all smiles as they shook hands with staff and politicians, making no distinction between the two. There was no sign of J.R. yet. He was probably still down in the Situation Room, being briefed on the attack, which he knew a lot more about than those briefing him.

I pulled the note out of my pocket and read it.

> Mr. President,
>
> I have Bethany. They wanted to take Will as well, but I hope I've prevented this. You must not tell anyone that Bethany has been kidnapped, as this will play right into the cell's

hands. If they can kidnap a member of the First Family from the White House, no one in the country is safe.

I may have talked to the man in charge tonight. This is a test of my loyalty and skill. If I pass it, I think he will identify himself to me. He claims to be Elise's older brother, which might lead you to his real identity.

Wayne Arbuckle is one of the moles. Another is a man named Conrad. By the time you read this, I will have taken both of these men out. If they are alive, you need to keep them both under wraps. I'll claim that they bungled the job and were either killed or captured. You can sweat them, but I don't think either of them knows anything about the cell except his own involvement in this plot. But there are still other unidentified moles on your staff that must have helped them get their jobs in the White House.

You will have to come up with a plausible cover story for Bethany's absence. Rest assured, I will protect her with my life as I protected yours when you were V.P. Before I let anything happen to her I will give up my cover and turn myself in.

I'll be in touch with you personally as soon as I can. I don't have a cell phone. They didn't want to risk the signal being tracked. But I will call your personal number as soon as I can.

Please trust me.

Malak Tucker

I read the note through twice and tried to imagine what J. R. Culpepper's reaction would be when he read it. Malak Tucker had decided to use his daughter as bait. I had a feeling that he was not going to be very happy with her.

I started to leave again but was stopped by my phone ringing. It was Angela.

"How many invitations did we give out?" she asked.

"Most people start out a phone conversation by saying something like, 'Hello.'"

"How many?"

"I didn't count them. Why?"

"There were supposed to be thirty."

"Right."

"Our list has only twenty-nine people on it."

Arbuckle. He pocketed one for himself. The reason he insisted that we send him the list was so he could add his "wife" to it. But I couldn't tell Angela this.

"Maybe the last invitation is stuck in your backpack somewhere," I said.

"The entire contents of my backpack are spread out on the floor. There is no blank invitation."

"Where are you?"

"I'm in the Library."

Perfect. There are 132 rooms in the White House (not counting the 35 bathrooms), and Angela is hiding out in the same room her mother is going to use to sneak the First Daughter outside and either knock out or kill Arbuckle.

"What about the missing invitation?" Angela asked.

"Maybe I didn't get all the names down," I said. "Or maybe we lost one of the invitations. Two of them could have gotten stuck together."

"Maybe," Angela said, but she didn't sound convinced.

I looked across the room. Mom and Roger were onstage now. Malak and Arbuckle were standing back from the stage, talking to Bethany Culpepper. Malak had waited until she was clear of Roger to approach the First Daughter. If I recognized Malak, he would recognize her, even with her disguise. I'd noticed that she wasn't wearing the gold necklace with the angel on it that Roger had given her. Even with the addition of the golden leopard next to the angel, that would have been a dead giveaway. Malak said something, and the three of them laughed.

"Are you there?" Angela asked.

"I'm here," I answered.

I needed to get to the kitchen and find P.K. It wasn't an itch, but I had an image of Chef Conrad chasing him around the cutting block with a meat cleaver. I also had to get Angela out of the Library.

"What about the invitation?" Angela said. "I have a feeling that Arbuckle kept one."

Good guess, sis.

"He might have. His wife is here. Maybe she badgered him into snatching one for her."

"His wife?"

"Yeah. I just talked to her. You'd like her." Angela was going to be really mad when this was all over and I told her the truth. "Why don't you meet me in the kitchen?"

"Why the kitchen?"

"I've got to help P.K. and Chef Conrad with the hors d'oeuvres. The guests are going through them faster than expected, and Conrad's having trouble keeping up."

"What do you know about making hors d'oeuvres?"

"Nothing. That's why I need you in the kitchen."

"I don't know anything about hors d'oeuvres."

"Conrad will show us, and so will the kitchen staff. If we don't help, P.K.'s going to miss the opening number."

"He doesn't work for Conrad."

"I know, but he says he owes him for some…"

Malak, Arbuckle, and Bethany had backed farther away from the stage. J. R. Culpepper walked through a side door, followed by Charlie Norton and a grim-looking Chief of Staff Todd.

"The president just came into the East Room. He's getting onstage to say something."

"Put your phone on speaker," Angela said.

"I need to get to the kitchen."

"Just do it, Q! I want to hear what he has to say. I'll come to the kitchen in a few minutes to help you."

"Fine." I hit the speaker button, set my iPhone on a windowsill, and headed for the kitchen.

Wayne Arbuckle was the man who had picked Malak up from the train station the night before. When he had put his arms around her as she entered the East Room she had asked if everything was ready. He'd said, "Yes." And that was the only conversation they'd had about the mission, which according to the man behind the light, had been in place for several years.

"We've just been waiting for the right time," he had told her. "This unscheduled concert is the perfect venue."

"You're lucky the president didn't cancel the concert because of the car bomb," Malak had said.

"Car bombs in several cities were scheduled to go off at the same time today. When I heard about the concert I aborted all of them, but it seems that Amun did not get the word or he disobeyed, not understanding why I aborted the attack. You are right about Amun being impulsive. I was furious with him, but now I'll never know whether he disobeyed or if there was a flaw in our communications."

"Did he know about your plans for the White House?"

"He knew there was going to be an attack on the White House, but he was not told what form it would take. Elise was to give him that information, providing her reservations about you were resolved.

"The man you will meet at the White House is called Wayne Arbuckle. He is inexperienced but committed, and has been preparing for this moment his entire adult life. We did not think the opportunity would come this soon. Our other man inside, Conrad Fournier, has assured me that everything is in place."

Malak looked at Arbuckle.

He was nervous but he was hiding it well, considering what they were about to do.

Bethany Culpepper was watching her father step onto the stage to loud applause. Malak hadn't seen her since Bethany was a teenager. When Arbuckle introduced them, there was a glimmer of recognition in the First Daughter's eyes, but it passed almost as fast as it had appeared, to Malak's relief. When Malak put on the wig, contacts, and makeup—turning herself into Mrs. Arbuckle— she did so with this meeting in mind. The man behind the light implored her to hurry with the disguise, insisting that no one would recognize her. She took her time. The man had no idea that she would be seeing people she had known and worked with for more than twenty years.

J.R. shook hands with Roger and Blaze. Roger looked good. In fact, he looked great. Malak couldn't help but feel a twinge of sadness at seeing him. They'd had some good times together, but even those had been overshadowed by her job with the Secret Service and his disapproval of her chosen profession.

J.R. began to speak.

"This has been a tragic day. Our prayers and thoughts go out to the victims of this cowardly..."

Malak tuned him out and scanned the room as she had been trained to do. The difference was that she was not looking for potential threats to the president. She was scanning for potential threats to herself and her mission. It was an odd sensation to be standing in a room she had stood in so many times before, viewing it as if she were on the other side of a mirror.

The Secret Service agents, and there were a lot of them tonight, also tuned the president out. Their job was not to listen to his words but to watch people's reactions to his words. If they saw someone or something that wasn't right, they would report it and move in closer. Most of the time it wasn't a threat at all, and if it was a threat, their proximity was usually enough to remove the threat. Malak was very careful to keep her expression and posture neutral so the agents did not move in on her.

Charlie Norton stood to the left of the stage with his back to the president, looking out at the crowd. A rumpled Pat Callaghan was standing to the right of the stage and appeared to be paying more attention to the tall blonde next to him than he was to the crowd or the president. Malak smiled. Pat was an excellent agent, but he had always liked the ladies. This had gotten him into a lot of trouble over the years.

Malak was too far back for either of them to see her clearly, which was intentional. She and Arbuckle had maneuvered Bethany to the back of the room. All they had to do now was to get her to move twenty feet to her right and they would have her in a perfect position.

"Some people have criticized me for not canceling this concert because of what happened today. But I have news for them and for the terrorists. This government, this society, is not intimidated by your actions..."

Malak continued looking around the room. She saw Q talking on a cell phone near the refreshment table and wondered why he hadn't gone to find P.K. If he didn't hurry, it would be too late. He set his cell phone down on the windowsill and rushed out of the room.

"I'm thirsty," Malak said.

"I'll get you something," Arbuckle said.

"No, I'll get it. Do you want anything, Bethany?"

"Please," Bethany said. "A glass of Chef Conrad's punch would be wonderful."

Arbuckle gave Malak a small frown. The plan was for him to get the First Daughter the glass of punch.

Change of plans, Malak thought. She gave her husband a peck on the cheek and walked over to the refreshment table.

Cold Trail

The assistant chefs and servers and dishwashers were all lined up quietly outside the East Room, down the hall from the State Dining Room, leaning against the wall listening to the president speak. P.K. and Conrad weren't with them.

I hurried through the pantry and to the kitchen. Conrad and P.K. weren't in the kitchen either. Except for the pots and pans and hors d'oeuvre trays, the kitchen was empty. I was too late. I opened all of the doors and cupboards even though I knew I wouldn't find anything. P.K. wasn't playing hide-and-seek—he'd been kidnapped. The last place I checked was the walk-in freezer. I pulled the heavy door open and pushed past the plastic strips hanging down to keep the cold air inside. The door closed behind me. The shelves were packed with ice cream, meat, fish, fruit, and dough. Sitting on a pallet in back was a replica of the White House in chocolate. But no P.K., no Chef Mole. I hurried back to the door and pushed the handle. The door didn't open. I pushed again, harder. Nothing.

Don't panic. There's probably a trick to opening the door from the inside.

I fished my flashlight out of one of my pockets and shined it on the mechanism. No trick. It was a simple push rod with a round end so the door could be swung open with your hip or butt if your hands were full. I stood back and gave the rod my best kick, slipped on the frosty floor, and nearly broke my leg.

I reached for my phone, doubting I'd get a signal, and then realized that I'd left it on the windowsill near the refreshment table.

Perfect! I lose the president's kid. I lock myself in a freezer. And I leave my only mode of communication on a windowsill.

I wasn't afraid of freezing to death. Eventually, someone would wander back into the kitchen. About every ten seconds I kicked the door handle. On about the fiftieth kick, the door flew open.

Angela was standing in the kitchen with her backpack slung over her shoulder, holding a long screwdriver.

"What's going on?" she asked.

Mom and Roger's beautiful music filled the kitchen. The concert had started.

"Why are you holding a screwdriver?"

"It was stuck through the door slot."

"Someone locked me in the freezer."

"P.K.?" Angela asked.

"No way. Chef Conrad."

"What's going on, Q?"

I think I was suffering from hypothermia because my brain didn't seem to be working at its normal speed.

"Why did you cut off the president's speech?"

"What?"

"Never mind," Angela said. "Just tell me what's going on."

"Chef Conrad is the mole," I said. "He's kidnapped P.K."

"Are you sure?"

"Do you think I'd make up something like that?"

"Let's get Boone or the Secret Service."

"We can't."

"Why?"

"There's no time. We have to find Conrad before he gets out of the house with P.K."

"If we tell the Secret Service, no one will get out of this house."

"You have to trust me, Angela. We cannot tell the Secret Service. We have to find P.K. on our own. Wait here a second."

I ran back upstairs and asked the chefs, servers, and dishwashers if they'd seen P.K. or Chef Conrad.

One of them told me that Conrad told them that he and P.K. had everything under control in the kitchen and to go out and enjoy the concert.

"He said he'd let us know when he needed us. Does he need us?"

I shook my head and headed back down to the kitchen.

"Which way did you come down here?" I asked Angela.

"I didn't come down here. The Library's on this same floor, right down the hall."

"Did you see any Secret Service agents?"

"One, walking down the hallway. Most of them are probably in the East Room."

"Didn't P.K. say there was a secret passage in the State

Dining Room leading down to the housekeeper's office?"

"He did."

"If you didn't see him, Conrad might be hiding P.K. in the passage until the coast is clear."

We ran across the hall to the housekeeper's office to look for the passage.

The Leopard did not own an MP3 player or an iPod. She liked music, but she didn't feel that she had time for that luxury in her present role. As a result, she had never heard Roger and Blaze sing.

She was stunned by the sound. During her time with the Secret Service she'd heard a dozen concerts in the East Room, but nothing like Match's.

Malak was having a hard time focusing on the mission. She found herself staring at the stage, watching Roger sing and play guitar. He had never sounded better. And Blaze's voice was a perfect match to his.

Bethany Culpepper had downed her punch like a sailor drinking rum. She was smiling. Her eyes were closed as she swayed to the music. The drug Malak had slipped into Bethany's drink was supposed to cause a sense of euphoria, detachment, and passivity.

As Malak looked around at the crowd, the people looked like they had all drunk the spiked punch, but their condition was caused by the music, not the drug.

"Maybe we should move over a few feet," Malak said. "I think we can get a better view of the stage."

Bethany didn't seem to care if she could see the stage or not.

Malak nodded at Arbuckle. They gently moved the swaying Bethany where they needed her to be. When they had her in position, Malak gave Arbuckle another nod. He took his cell phone out and hit a series of numbers. The lights went out and the music stopped. The emergency power kicked in, and the lights came back on, but just for a second.

Arbuckle hit another series of numbers. The room went black and stayed that way.

Blackout

The music stopped.

I turned on my flashlight and continued looking for the secret passage, which I had narrowed down to a small hollow-sounding area inside the linen closet. *Tap-tap-tap* with the butt of the screwdriver Conrad had used to lock me in the freezer. He must have stepped outside the kitchen with P.K. when I walked in and waited for me to step into the freezer.

I'd wondered how they planned to get P.K. and Bethany out of the White House. Now I knew—secret passages and the cover of darkness. But why hadn't P.K. called out? What had Conrad done to silence him?

"This must be it," Angela said. "It's the only hollow wall. The latch has to be here."

Angela had barely jumped when the lights went out. After I'd asked her to trust me she hadn't asked for any more details. She had stayed focused on finding the passage, pursuing Chef Conrad, and saving P.K.

Trust needs to be rewarded with trust.

"Your mother is okay," I said.

There was a sigh of relief in the darkness. "How do you know?"

"She's here...or she was here. Arbuckle's the other mole. She posed as his wife. You were right. He copped the missing invitation. They're kidnapping Bethany Culpepper. Malak wants us to let her get away with it. She gave me a note for the president. She promises to protect Bethany with her life. I suspect they are on their way out of the White House. She told me not to tell you because she was afraid that your reaction would give her away. She didn't want to see you because she was afraid that *her* reaction would give her away."

Angela started to cry but continued groping for the secret latch.

Click.

A panel slid back. I wasn't sure if I'd discovered the latch or if Angela had accidentally hit it, and I didn't care. We climbed through the opening. The panel slid closed behind us. There must have been a pressure plate on the floor.

"We'll need to be quiet," Angela whispered. "If Conrad knows we're on his trail, he might hurt P.K. Which way?"

The passage was much bigger than I thought it would be. There was enough room for us to stand without hitting our heads. I shined the flashlight at my feet. Thick dust. No footprints. Conrad and P.K. had not gotten this far, or they weren't coming this way.

Tyrone Boone was standing in the dark to the right of the stage on a conference call to X-Ray with Charlie Norton and Pat Callaghan. Norton and Callaghan were standing next to him.

"Any idea how they pulled the plug?" Boone asked X-Ray.

"The White House is not the only building down," X-Ray answered. "Somehow they got to the electrical grid."

"What's more surprising is that they managed to shut down the backup system," Norton said. "Whoever figured that out had access to the electrical panels and the generators, which are under guard 24-7."

"They'll get the primary power up pretty quickly," X-Ray said.

"I haven't seen Vanessa," Boone said. "Is she here?"

"No. She's flying the drone. We thought it would be better to get it up in the air than for her to go to a party."

Someone came up and tapped Boone on the shoulder. It was Ziv, aka Warren Parker. He looked at Norton and Callaghan.

"I have to go," Boone said, ending the call. He looked at Ziv and nodded at Charlie and Pat. "They're on the SOS team."

"The Leopard is here," Ziv said quietly.

"Where?"

"I lost her when the lights went out, but she was standing in the back with Bethany Culpepper and a man."

"Wayne Arbuckle," Norton said. "He's Bethany's new assistant. He's been glued to her all evening. I saw the woman with him and assumed she was Arbuckle's wife or girlfriend. She didn't look anything like Malak."

"Of course not," Ziv said.

"Any ideas why she's here?" Boone asked.

"No," Ziv answered. "But I saw her kiss the man on the cheek, then walk over to get a drink for Bethany."

"Any Secret Service around Bethany?"

"No."

"There wouldn't be," Pat said. "She was with her assistant—no potential threat."

"We need to find them," Norton said.

"If you see the Leopard," Ziv said, "do not approach her. She will let us know if she needs our help."

The power came back on.

Boone, Charlie, and Pat blinked to adjust to the sudden light. When they opened them Ziv was gone.

The Library

We didn't find Chef Conrad. He found us.

He was hiding in a small alcove inside the secret passage, and we walked right by him. He stepped out behind us, holding a butcher knife in one hand and P.K. with the other hand.

"Hey, guys," P.K. said with a goofy grin, seemingly unaware that a terrorist chef was holding him at knifepoint. "Me and Cheesy are exploring."

"You okay, P.K.?" I asked, hoping Angela knew how to disarm a chef wielding a butcher knife with tae kwon do.

"I feel great!" P.K. said.

"You drugged him," Angela said.

"That's right," Chef Conrad said. "And I will kill him if you two don't do as I say."

"What do you want us to do?" Angela said.

"Go back the way you came. I'll be right behind you with P.K."

We turned around and started back down the passage with

Angela in the lead. When we got to the panel, Chef Conrad told us to stop.

"Step on the pressure plate."

Angela stepped on it and the panel slid open. The lights were back on.

We walked through the opening. P.K. was a little unsteady. His usually bright and alert green eyes were dull and unfocused.

"We will walk to the Library together," Conrad said. "If we happen to come across anyone and you raise an alarm, I will kill your friend. No one will be able to stop me in time. And if you think I fear for my life, you are wrong. I will gladly die after killing this boy."

P.K. actually laughed. Apparently, he hadn't heard the same thing we'd just heard.

We started down the hallway to the Library.

No one was there, which was a relief. If a Secret Service agent saw the four of us walking down the hallway, we wouldn't have to raise an alarm. The agent would be alarmed and ask us what we were doing.

We stepped into the Library, and Chef Conrad closed the door behind us. It was a beautiful room with floor-to-ceiling cases filled with books. Angela calmly focused on Chef Conrad. I'd seen the look before outside the hospital emergency room in Philadelphia, just before she took out Eben Lavi and the woman he was with. The difference was that Eben didn't have a knife in his hand or a hostage.

"Don't do it, Angela," I said.

She frowned. "What are you talking about?"

"You know what I'm talking about. Trust me. Don't do it."

"Do what?" Chef Conrad asked.

"Angela is a black belt in tae kwon do."

"Are you crazy, Q?" Angela shouted.

I knew something she didn't know. The Library was missing something, but I couldn't tell her what it was in front of Chef Conrad.

"Keep your voice down," Conrad said.

"What now?" I asked.

"You two sit."

We sat next to each other on a small sofa. I could feel the heat of Angela's anger coming off her body.

One of the bookcases to our left swung open. The first person through was a dusty Wayne Arbuckle. He was followed by Bethany and Mrs. Arbuckle.

I put my hand on Angela's knee and squeezed as hard as I could. This got her attention off Mrs. Arbuckle, who was in fact her mother.

"What are they doing here?" Malak said to Conrad. "This wasn't part of the plan."

"Hi, Bethany," P.K. said happily.

"Hi, Willingham," Bethany said with the same goofy grin on her face that he had.

"They stumbled across me," Conrad said. "I thought we might take them with us. Their parents are two of the most famous people on earth right now. Twice the impact. If you don't want to take them, we can kill them right here."

"That's not a bad idea," Malak said. "Give me your knife."

Conrad handed it to her. Malak turned to Arbuckle. "What do you think?"

"It won't be easy getting out of here with four hostages," he answered.

"I agree."

Malak hit Arbuckle in the throat with her fist, then kicked him in the knee.

Conrad pushed P.K. to the side and lunged for Malak, but Angela was off the sofa like a bullet, using a vicious combination of hand and foot blows. He crumpled to the ground and was out for the count in less than five seconds.

"You've been practicing," Malak said.

"A little," Angela said.

"A lot." Malak crossed the room and gave her a hug and a kiss on her forehead. "This will be over soon. I need to go." She looked at me. "Do you have the note?"

"Right here."

"You need to get to J.R. right away. Have Norton or Callaghan tell him what's going on and pass him the note. The agents won't let Boone within fifty feet of the president. I need five minutes. You might want to tie these guys up before you leave here. We can't have them wandering around the White House."

She pointed to Angela's pack. "You wouldn't happen to have any rope in there?"

"No," Angela said. "But Q has a pocketful of tricks. We'll tie them up."

Malak took Bethany by the hand and led her to a bookcase on the opposite side of the room. She pulled out a book and pushed something behind it. The case swung open.

"Whoa, another secret passage," P.K. said.

Malak looked at Angela. "I love you."

"I love you too," Angela said.

"Bye, P.K.," Bethany said.

"Bye, sis," P.K. said. "Have fun."

Malak and Bethany stepped through the opening, and the bookcase closed behind them.

I reached into a pocket and pulled out a few lengths of cord that I used for magic tricks. I tossed one to Angela.

"You knew she was coming down here," Angela said.

"Not exactly. She said that we would find Arbuckle dead or unconscious in the Library. He wasn't here, so I figure she'd make a deposit before she left."

"Is he dead?"

I went over and took a look at him. "No, but he's going to have a sore throat when he wakes up."

Debriefing

The concert had resumed and was still going on, but Angela and I were two floors above, sitting in the Solarium with Boone and a very angry, very distraught J. R. Culpepper. He was holding Malak's crumpled note in his hand. Norton and Callaghan had gone down to the Library to get Arbuckle and Conrad out of the White House before anyone discovered them. P.K. was in his bed, sound asleep.

"Do we have any idea where Bethany is?" J.R. asked.

"Not yet," Boone said. "But we'll find her. We had the drone up in the air over the area. Callaghan and Norton are taking Arbuckle and Conrad out the same way Malak took Bethany. When they exit we'll be able to back the surveillance footage up and zero in on her. She had to have a car waiting."

J.R. shook his head and held the note up. "I'm not sure I can go through with this, Boone. It might be time to call in the cavalry."

"It's your daughter," Boone said. "Your call."

"What do you think?"

"I think she's safe with Malak."

"Malak used Bethany!" J.R. said angrily. "They drugged two of my children!" He closed his eyes and took a deep breath.

Boone let him settle down, then said, "You have terrorists working in the White House. They could have easily killed P.K. and Bethany. Malak saved them both with some help from Angela and Q."

"What am I going to tell the media?"

"Tell them that Bethany had a nervous collapse and has been taken to an undisclosed location to recover. Malak's right. If anyone finds out that Bethany's been kidnapped from the White House, the ghost cell wins. If they can get in here, they can get in anywhere."

"I want the SOS team on this full time until Bethany's back," J.R. said.

"That could be a bit of a problem," Boone said. "I promised Malak that I would protect Angela and Q and Roger and Blaze. I can't do that if I'm not with them."

J.R. thought about this for a minute. "You have security on Roger and Blaze?"

"Yeah. Marie and Art, their personal assistants, work for me. But it's hard for two people to guard four people."

J.R. looked at me and Angela. "Then let's split them up. I'll tell Roger and Blaze that I need them to spend another night here and do a joint press conference with me about the victim fund. I'll have them flown on Air Force One to their next concert. You, Angela, and Q will leave by motor coach tonight. But of course you won't be going to the next concert.

You're going to find Bethany."

Boone looked at us. "You think your parents will go for that?"

Angela nodded. "We can talk them into it."

J.R.'s cell phone buzzed. He looked at the screen and then looked at me. "Is this a joke?"

"What are you talking about?"

"It says I have a text message from you."

I patted my pockets, then remembered. "I left my phone down in the East Room."

"You didn't put my private number in your contacts, did you?"

"Of course not," I said. "It's on the back of my watch."

J.R. hit a button and read the text. " 'Bethany is safe. I'll be in touch. Malak.' "

"She took my phone," I said.

Boone pulled his BlackBerry out and hit the tracking icon.

"She's on I-95, headed south," he said.

J.R. nodded. "Get her back, Boone."

MLib